Bill's Secret Wise Man

Bill's Secret Wise Man

Ron J. Hammond

RockyRidge Press
Payson, Utah

Printed and bound in the United States of America.

All characters in this story are fictional. Any resemblance to real persons, assumed or implied, is strictly coincidental.

First printing 2003

ISBN 0-9740512-0-9

LCCN 2003095423

Cover art produced by: Aspen Graphics, 360 West 400 North #26, Springville, Utah, 84663
Front cover photo: Winter Mountain Road © 2003 Dean Johnson
Rear cover photo: Winter Academy © 2003 Dean Johnson
Both photographs used by permission of Dean Johnson
Typeset by Marny K. Parkin

To order more copies of *Bill's Secret Wise Man,* send a check or money order for $11.99 + $2.00 shipping to:
RockyRidge Press
PO Box 345
Payson, Utah 84651-345
10% discounts on ten or more copies

THIS STORY is dedicated to all the Bills and all the loving people who care for them.

Someday, we'll know why we suffered from the darkness. Until then . . . here's to our hope in the final outcome.

Acknowledgment

I EXPRESS my sincere gratitude to Dorothy Bryson and Ingrid Perkins for their courage and strength in enduring the caregiving of their late husbands and for reopening the wounds, so to speak, in order to teach me about their experiences. Thanks to Esther Mauss for finishing the race and finishing with dignity in her care of Grandpa Mauss. Thanks to JoAnn Harris, who made all this possible. Thanks to Katy Olson, Allison Smith, Katie Anderton, Janae Olson, and Paul Robertson. Thanks to Becky and her mother, Nancy McClellan, for their courageous feedback and support. Thanks to Russ Bennett, Kate and Janae Olsen, Koh, Kyung-Ran, Denise Barney and Anne Denise Robinson, Renae Bastean and Andrea Close, and Sam Durst. Thanks to Julie Bellon who exceeded all my expectations in her reviews of my novels. Thanks to Valene Tuttle, Lee Ann Setzer, Carol Morgan, Barbara Bearnson. Thanks to Dean and Angie Johnson, good friends and truly a class act. Thanks to Paul and Lolly Penrod who own Roe's Bake Shop and felt excited about it being part of these characters's lives. Thanks to Lynne and Gary Hammond. Thanks also to Matt Lohrke for encouragement and observation under fire. I express my greatest appreciation to my wife Alisa, who has yet to read a story of mine empty handed (to the betterment of the story I might add).

Contents

One: José's Gifts 11
Two: Lost in Room 1225 29
Three: The Wilson Family Assignment 39
Four: Memory Recovery Specialist .51
Five: Fat-Free Sugar-Free Hot Chocolate 59
Six: Christmas Photo Album 67
Seven: Sausage, Pancakes, and Syrup 79
Eight: Jacob and His Dad 87
Nine: What's Up, Bill? 95
Ten: Christmas Cabin 101
Eleven: Christmas Morning 117

☙ One ❧

José's Gifts

BILL SLOWED his small plane as he approached Payson Municipal airport from the south. Over the last thirty years, he'd landed here hundreds of times, but never through such an unyielding blizzard like this. Snow covered most of his windshield. The storm clouds had made it impossible to see anything out the windows for the last distressing hour. Beyond that, nightfall and thick cloud cover churned past the lights on his wings. To make matters even worse, strong winds pounded him from the right. The sleek fiberglass-bodied plane careened to port with each gust. He constantly muscled the controls to keep on course.

"Tower, this is Bravo 1223. Come in." Bill's breath fogged as he rechecked his compass and global navigation system. They both indicated he flew north. Static interference broke the silence in his headset.

"Tower, this is Bravo 1223. Come in. Do you read me?" He searched frantically out of his port then starboard windows for any landmarks. *Thud!* An exceptionally strong burst of wind smashed into his starboard side, whirling the plane onto its left wing, the right wing pointing to the sky.

Duuut! Duuut! Duuut! The crash warning alarm screamed in his headset, adding more strain to his untenable situation.

Duuut! Duuut! Duuut! Bill knew he only had seconds to recover at this low altitude. He took in a deep chest full of air and leaned his entire body against the force of the roll, clinching his jaw, pulling the stick hard right, and pressing full force into the accelerator pedal.

Duuut! Duuut! . . . The alarm quit as the plane leveled back out.

Altitude two hundred feet. He rechecked the instruments. Still flying north. Good airspeed. Ten miles to the airport. And zero forward visibility.

"Payson tower, be advised, this is Bravo 1223, requesting immediate clearance to land at Payson municipal airport. Do you read me?" Bill's voice sounded serious, but not desperate. He knew any indication of his peril would get back to his family by word of mouth. He didn't want to burden them. His windshield wipers hesitated as they strained against the hard-packed snow.

"Come on," he moaned. "I've made it this far." He pounded the windshield with his fist but still couldn't see out. The low fuel indicator on the dash flashed a red warning light.

He pounded the windshield again and a large snow chunk flew off, revealing the runway lights about one mile out in front of him. Just then, a gurgled voice came into his headset. Bill turned the volume up to its max.

"Payson tower, I have your runway in my sights and am requesting immediate clearance to land."

"Bravo 1223, this is Payson tower. . . . Is that you?"

"Yes!" Bill screamed. "I mean, 10-4, Payson tower. The Santa express is coming in for a landing." His shoulders ached, his hands felt numb, and his neck and head pounded from the worst tension headache he'd ever had.

"Bravo 1223, be advised, condition at Payson municipal airport is level red. Repeat level red. This is worst blizzard we've ever recorded."

"It's been a real adventure. I'll tell you about it after I get on the ground." Bill checked his altitude. It read just under one hundred feet as he descended toward the runway.

"10-4, Bravo 1223, you have permission to land on runway two-niner. But could you circle the airport while the crew plows the runway? We've had a foot of snow in the last hour."

"Payson tower, be advised, I am running low on fuel. Requesting immediate . . ." The engine died, dropping the plane fifty feet in only a few terrifying seconds. Bill gripped the stick with both hands, pulling back to keep the nose up. His plane smashed down hard into the snow-covered runway.

It bounced up again, glided thirty feet, then dropped again onto its wheels, slamming Bill's forehead into the port-side window. It skidded straight down the runway, plowing snow into waves on both sides. The force jolted him back and forth inside his harness.

After plowing half the length of the runway, the plane came to a halt. The wiper blade squeaked across the windshield, cleared by the force of the impact.

The wind howled outside. Bill released the stick, removed his gloves, then pressed the harness release button. His strength gone, he slumped motionless back into his seat. The left side of his head pounded with each beat of his heart.

Got to relax. He took a deep breath and let it slowly escape through his lips. He thought about his sweet wife, waiting for him at the hospital and tried to imagine how her clown outfit turned out. This made him think about José. Only two years earlier, José came into Bill's office as his last appointment of the day, clutching his aunts hand as she practically dragged him up to the examination table and pleaded, "Can you please help my little José? He is sick."

Bill lost that mental image as he thought of the now-emaciated nine-year-old José he'd seen yesterday, lying frail in the hospital bed.

"Bravo 1223, are you all right?" The radio clicked on, jarring him from his thoughts.

"10-4, Payson tower. Be advised that fuel was running low, had to land right away. Request assistance into the hangar."

"Bravo 1223, that has to be the cleanest, most daring landing I've ever seen." Bill slightly raised his eyebrows. It made his head hurt. "And you landed in over a foot of snow . . . Unbelievable!"

"10-4. Could you send a tug out to the plane and tow me into the hangar?"

"Bravo 1223, 10-4, tug is on its way." The tow vehicle darted out of the hangar, plowing it's own path through the snow. It stopped in front of Bravo 1223. A crewman ran up to the cockpit. He waved both fists over his head in victory dance even though the snow and wind pounded him. Bill smiled and waved back, but he didn't share in the celebration. He rarely bragged. He just wanted to meet his wife and deliver his Christmas cargo. The plane jolted, then followed the tow vehicle.

"Thank you, Lord. This means the world to me," he whispered, looking upward. "Now, I know I've asked a great deal so far, but could you help me finish our plans for José?" Bill interlocked his fingers as he prayed.

The crewman towed the plane from the storm into the safety of the spacious hangar. Bill watched the large mechanical hangar doors close behind the plane. He saw a young woman, standing next to his green Suburban, parked in the rear of the hangar. *Elizabeth is so dependable*.

She stood bundled in a large winter coat, waiving and smiling to him. Bill opened the side door and stepped down quickly. He smiled, waved back, then grabbed his flight bag from the front passenger seat, draping the strap over his shoulder.

"Ouch!" His forehead stung as he moved around. In his mirror, he discovered a monstrous swollen red bump on his forehead. It contrasted his greyish white hair but went well with his Santa costume, which he had worn during the flight back home. "I can't have that showing." He quickly threw on his oversized Santa cap. It looked like any other Santa cap except he'd sewn grey rabbit ears on each side of it. He retrieved a large cardboard box from behind his seat and sat it on the hangar floor.

"Tower just said they caught that landing on security cameras. You're going to be famous." The crewman announced excitedly as he shook Bill's hand.

"Oh, boy." Bill worried his wife would somehow end up seeing it.

"What, sir?"

"Nothing. Thanks for the tow."

"No problem, sir. Hey, uh, why the Santa outfit?" The crewman looked Bill over head to toe.

"I'm playing Santa Claus to one of the children in the hospital in a few minutes."

"That's cool."

"Oh, I'll be flying again next week; can you fill her up and give her a full inspection for my next flight?" Bill shook his hand again, this time leaving a fifty dollar bill with him.

"Yes, sir! She'll be ship-shape for your next flight." The crewman nodded as he hurried about his work.

"Merry Christmas."

"You, too, sir." he replied without looking back to see Bill's smile.

"Santa!" Elizabeth scolded.

"Yes." Bill spun around to find her standing with both hands on her hips.

"If your sweet wife knew you had landed in a storm like this, she'd have your pilot's license."

"Elizabeth . . ." Bill shook his head. "That's why I pay you so much to be my receptionist—you know how to keep professional confidences." Bill walked past her to file his flight papers at the desk. Elizabeth retrieved the cardboard box, put it in the back seat, then sat in the driver's seat of the Suburban. Bill climbed in on the passenger's side. "On to the hospital," he exclaimed, hoping to distract her.

"Professional confidences, my eye." She finally smiled. Bill chuckled. She drove out the exit into the storm. The windshield wipers worked full-speed, barely keeping the windshield clear of snow. He continued his efforts at relaxation.

"The hospital called today. José is stable after his chemo."

"Is he conscious?"

"Yes. His nurse said he handled this chemotherapy much better than the last."

"Good."

"She also said he's weak. But guess what!"

"What?"

"He actually carried on a conversation with her—something about Santa Bunny and a Christmas clown named Squeaky, coming to see him tonight. If you ask me, he's one lucky kid to have a doctor like you."

"Funny, I feel lucky to have him as my patient. José is a real big hero in a tiny little body, isn't he?"

"Yeah, I don't know how I'd handle three surgeries and three rounds of chemo." Elizabeth turned onto the frontage road. Bill thought about what she'd said as they slowly approached town.

"Things went well at the office today?"

"Yes, we only had three mothers call in for refills on their children's prescriptions. The nurses handled that."

"That's typical. Children don't stop being sick just because it's the holidays." As they approached the main red light, he took in the beauty of the familiar lights and garlands on the trees, lamp posts, and store fronts.

Elizabeth waited at the green light while a horse-drawn sleigh passed. He watched the young couple riding in the sleigh, cuddled together under the same blanket. The young man held an umbrella against the snow, the young women rested her head on his shoulder beneath its protection. They looked totally absorbed in each other and oblivious to the storm. Bill had seen their wedding announcement in the paper last week. They'd be married tomorrow. He smiled, finally feeling some relief.

"Your wife, I mean Squeaky, is so cute in her clown outfit."

"She's cute in anything she wears." Bill continued to watch the sleigh as it turned up main street into the historic district. "Did she get her clown shoes today?"

"Yes, they came in the UPS shipment, along with a few of

her late presents you've been waiting for."

"Did one have an Ohio return address?"

"Yes, it was real heavy, too." Elizabeth slowly pulled away from the intersection and headed up the hill toward the hospital.

"Hyrum Farms real maple syrup. It's her favorite."

"That's right. Well, I put it with the other packages in the back seat. You can sneak them under your tree later tonight." Elizabeth soon drove into the hospital's parking garage. She parked in a space marked *Silly Wabbit* above a picture of Bill wearing his grey rabbit ears. He'd had that sign made special because his young patients loved the bunny persona he used to set them at ease. She turned off the ignition then checked her watch.

"Two minutes early. You must have had angels flying with you." Elizabeth handed Bill his keys. He didn't take them.

"Angels." He felt a warm feeling send chills up his arms. It surprised him that he hadn't recognized it before now.

"What's the matter?" She showed him his keys in her open hand. "Are you all right?"

"Angels, that's right. I must have had angels with me." He took his keys, stepped out into the parking garage, opened the back door, and reached into the box that he'd brought on the plane. He'd brought presents for all his office staff.

"I'm parked a few stalls down. I better get going. My husband and I are spending Christmas with his parents in Wyoming," Elizabeth said, standing behind him as he searched the box.

"This is for you, Elizabeth." He handed her a present.

"You didn't have to bring me a gift, but thank you." She unwrapped it to discover a foot-tall statue. She smiled as she examined it. "It's the statue of Jesus, standing with his arms ready to give a hug. I've always wanted one of these. Thank you so much!"

"You're welcome. I got it from an importer. It's hand-carved in a small village outside of Mexico City."

"Thank you, again." Elizabeth's eyes glistened as she cradled the statue in her arms.

"You're very welcome. Oh, I almost forgot." He reached back into the box. "This is for you and your husband." Bill handed her a round loaf of bread and a large rectangle of chocolate. "The sourdough bread was baked fresh today. And this five pound chocolate bar was bought fresh today, both at Fisherman's Wharf. Merry Christmas, Elizabeth, to you, your husband, and his parents."

"You are so thoughtful." Elizabeth's tender expression communicated her feelings of appreciation. "We already got your Christmas bonus check yesterday. All this is more than I deserve as your receptionist." She adjusted the statue, bread, and chocolate in her arms.

"Christmas is like that for all of us. It's more than we deserve, but we get it anyway."

"Merry Christmas, Santa Bunny. To you, your wife and your family." She walked toward her car. He waited for her to drive out of the garage, waved one last time, then rushed to the front of the Suburban, grabbing a handful of wet snow from the bumper. His bump stung fiercely as he slowly removed his Santa cap. He looked in the side-view mirror to find it had doubled in size. It looked like half a big red apple, growing out of his head.

He gently placed a handful of dripping snow onto the bump. The intense cold made him jerk his shoulders up toward his neck. His headache worsened. Still holding the snow onto his head, he reached into his flight bag and retrieved two aspirin. He swallowed them without any water, flung the snow to the ground, gently wiped his forehead with his sleeve, then replaced his Santa cap. He attached his Santa beard to the sides of the cap which made the spring-loaded grey floppy bunny ears on his cap jiggle. He then took a small Christmas present from the flight bag, grabbed another large thin present, and shut the door.

"Hyuk, yuk, yuk!" he said in a goofy voice as he watched his reflection in the car window. He jogged toward the hospital door at the end of the garage.

He loved this hospital. He'd treated his patients here for over thirty years. As the senior physician, he'd watched it change and grow over the years. The center portion once served as a public school called the Peteetneet Academy, built over a hundred years earlier. Peteetneet came from native tribes in the region.

Once a school, then a museum, and now a hospital, it sat on the crest of a large hill. It's antique tan bricks covered most of its exterior. The deep red sandstone used for the arches above some of the windows and doors stood out sharply against the color of the bricks. On both the east and west sides stood two modern additions.

Bill entered through the east addition. He had to use his key at this late hour because the door lead to the maternity ward. *Warmth, finally,* he thought as he unbuttoned his winter coat. The digital clock on the wall read 8:01 P.M.

Uh oh, I'm a minute late now, but I do have to stop at the nursery, just for a minute. He did, recognizing two little boy patients, born yesterday. They slept peacefully in their tiny beds.

He made himself leave, walking on through the old academy section. It had to be the most beautiful emergency room in the world. The entry way had double doors on its north and south sides. The original hardwood floors sounded each step he took. He noticed the Christmas lights that decorated both sets of stairs that ascended on the north and south up to the second floor. A third set ascended between the other two from the second floor to the third.

He continued on into the corridor that lead to the brain trauma wing. In the last room at the far end of this wing, he found the one and only pediatric intensive care unit.

The hospital didn't really have a pediatric intensive care unit. They improvised because José wanted to stay close to his Aunt Maria here in Payson as long as his treatment allowed for it. Bill sat the thin present against the wall. He opened the door. He saw one bed with a small nine-year-old boy. José's small tan frame, round cheeks, big brown eyes, and bald head stirred Bill's feelings.

"Hello, doctor," a middle-aged nurse said. Bill closed the door and turned. "Squeaky the Clown is in the ladies' room touching up her makeup."

"Thank you, nurse. How's José doing right now?"

"Stable, thank the good Lord. Would you like to see his charts?"

"Not right now." He looked at his watch.

"I think you are the only Santa Claus I've ever seen with grey bunny ears on your head." She stood back and looked at his costume. "You know, José asked me earlier if Santa Bunny was coming to see him again like he did last year."

"He did?" They both smiled.

"Doctor, it makes me feel sad to tell you . . ."

His smile disappeared. "Tell me what?"

"I just received a call. Tomorrow they're transferring José to the Huntsman Cancer Center at 7:00 A.M. Since today's chemo was the last procedure we can offer José, they put him higher on their priority list."

"Oh?" Bill looked down at the floor.

"I'm sorry. I know how much you care for him."

"I will sorely miss him." He knew just how low José's chances for survival had become. It saddened him to see any child suffer. It nearly broke him to watch José under the ravages of cancer.

"Bill, you made it!"

"Safe and sound." He received a big hug and kiss from his wife. The sweet smell of her perfume felt comforting.

"I worried about you so much." The rim of her clown's hat pressed against his forehead. He grimaced. "Well, what do you think about Squeaky?" She stepped back, holding both arms out and turning a circle.

"I think she must be as sexy as the day I first met her." He raised both eyebrows.

"Oh, Santa, you find this attractive, huh?" She gripped the bike horns sewn like two pistols to the hips of her outfit.

Nyank! one blew. *Nyonk!* the other blew. *Nyank, nyonk, nyonk nyonk, nyank, nyank!*

"That's pretty good." He hugged her. "I love you, sweetheart." He whispered in a suggestive tone.

"Excuse me. I think I'll leave you two alone now." The nurse retreated to her station.

"Oh, Santa." A gleam of innocense radiated from her eyes. "First things first. Did you get them?"

"Yep."

"Can we go give them to José?"

"After a kiss." Bill gently pressed his lips against hers.

Nyank, nyonk! She squeaked the horns. "Time's up," she softly whispered, gave him one more peck, then pulled him by the hand to José's door. Bill retrieved the thin present, carrying both gifts as Squeaky slowly opened the door. José didn't notice them in his room at first.

"Hyuk, yuk, yuk!" Santa announced. José slowly turned his head. He smiled once he saw them, but his weak smile couldn't conceal his suffering. Bill noticed the oxygen tube and IV.

"What's up, Doc?" José raised a few fingers off the mattress in an attempt to wave.

"You, ya silly wabbit," Santa replied cheerfully. "I'll tell you what's up. Squeaky the Clown and I are looking for our favorite friend, José. Have you seen him around?" José let out a single laugh.

"Yeah, howdy!" Squeaky called in a loud, cowboy-type accent. "We's got some Christmas gifts that Santa Claus asked us to deliver in person to a special boy named José. Have ya seen him here, little boy?" Squeaky danced in a circle. Her arms pumped up and down her side as her body wobbled left and right and her eighteen inch shoes slapped with each step. Santa smiled, surprised by Squeaky's new talents.

"Me."

"You?" they both asked.

"You mean, you're José?" Santa asked excitedly. José nodded once.

"This whole time he's been right here in front of us." Squeaky took the small present from Santa as they wobbled to opposite sides of the bed.

"José, we've got some very special gifts for you." José's eyebrows raised slightly. "Ya see, whipper snapper."

Nyank, nyonk, nyonk. José smiled again.

"Your Grandma and Grandpa, your ma and pa, and your cousins." She bent down to whisper. "We found out about them from your Aunt Maria. She directed old Santa Bunny here to fly down to San Francisco, California."

"You flew to San Francisco, Santa?" José looked over to him. "Was the team practicing for the Super Bowl?"

"Yes, sir, I did and yes, sir, they were."

"In fact, Santa just got back into Payson a few minutes ago. And he brought you a very special present this year." Squeaky placed the small box into José's little hand.

"Before you open it, I need to tell you that this may very well be the best Christmas present in the world, José." Santa explained.

"Why?" José looked at the small red-wrapped box.

"Because it was sent with all the love of your family and friends. As long as you wear it, you can feel their love in your heart."

"Really?"

"Really."

José opened the paper quickly. Santa had wrapped it very loose since José had little strength. Inside the box, lay a necklace and gold medallion. Squeaky took them from the box and placed the necklace gently around José's neck. José lifted it up, staring at the medallion.

"Jesus!" He announced.

"Can you feel it, José?" Santa leaned down to whisper.

"Feel what?"

"Feel the love of all your family and friends in your heart?"

"Yes. And I feel Jesus' love, too. He's my friend, you know," José explained. "He told me so, last year." Santa and Squeaky glanced at one another.

"If Jesus told you that, then it must be true." Santa gently laid his hand onto José's.

"Just keep that with ya always, and no matter what happens, you'll feel all our love, partner." Squeaky smiled. "But wait, boys. We ain't done yet." Squeaky danced in a circle again.

Nyank, nyonk, nyonk, nyonk, nyonk, nyank, nyank!

"We ain't? I mean, we're not?" Santa asked with over-dramatized interest.

"Oh, thar's another big present from Californy."

"There is?" Santa and José asked.

"Well, where is it?" Santa looked around.

"Santa," José whispered, pulling on his red sleeve. "I think you're holding it."

"I am?"

"Yes." José nodded twice. Bill looked down at his hand.

"You mean this?" He pointed to the big present. José's eye widened.

"Oh, I can't give you this." Santa shook his head, looking into José's eyes. José stopped smiling, but his eyes remained wide open.

"You see . . ." Squeaky joined in the suspense-building. "This is for the best Steve Young fan in the world."

"That's me." José's smile returned.

"You?" Santa and Squeaky asked.

"Well, there ya go!" Squeaky snapped her fingers. Santa slowly brought the gift in front of José who reached up and pulled the ribbon, releasing the wrapping paper and revealing the framed poster.

"Steve Young in his football uniform!" José exclaimed. "Thank you! Thank you!" José clasped both hands together in excitement. I've always wanted a poster of Steve Young. He's the best football player in the universe, you know."

"Well, José, Steve Young waited for two hours in the San Francisco airport to make sure he gave this to me personally. He asked me to give it to you for him."

"To me?"

"Yes, look down here." Santa pointed to the bottom corner of the poster. José gasped.

"Read it, partner, I can't read much without my glasses."

"It says . . ."

To the best fan in the world.
You get better and I'll come to see you.
Te amo mucho, amigo.
Steve Young

"Muchas gracias, Santa y Squeaky." José reached out to touch the signature.

"De nada," they replied.

"Merry Christmas, José." Squeaky gently kissed his forehead.

"Merry Christmas." Santa kissed his hand.

"This is the best Christmas ever." José looked up into Santa's then Squeaky's eyes.

"For us, too, partner." Squeaky softly replied, speaking in a loving tone.

"We'll miss seeing you every day, little man." Bill whispered. "Tomorrow you go up to the center."

"I do?"

"Yes. But your Mamá and Papá already drove up to their new apartment. They had to get things ready for you," said Bill. José's bottom lip poked out and his eyes looked down at his feet.

"What's the matter?" Santa whispered. José didn't answer.

"Tell us what's on your mind, little man." Squeaky caressed his head.

"I feel sad."

"Why? We'll see you every chance we get." Santa smiled

big trying to get him to smile. José didn't.

"I know. But . . ."

"But what, José?" Squeaky encouraged.

"But I didn't get you any presents for Christmas."

"Oh, but Christmas is about doing for others. We feel happy because we could do this for you. Does that make sense?" Santa asked. José pondered what he'd said as he held his picture of Jesus in his hand. "I tell you what, José. Why don't you get me a Christmas gift."

"Really, you'll let me?"

"Sure, you think about it and maybe find something you could do for me, something that cost no money." José nodded. Squeaky joined Santa next to the IV stand.

"Squeaky, Santa, please remember me." José's little eyes closed about half-way.

"We will, José."

"Te amo mucho, amigo." Santa rubbed his hand as he placed it down on the bed.

"Te amo, Squeaky and Doc. I mean Santa Bunny." Squeaky propped the poster beside José's bed. José slowly placed his fingers on it as he closed his eyes all the way.

Squeaky and Santa walked out into the hall hand in hand past the nurses station toward the ER. Neither could talk. Bill sat down at the administrator's desk in the middle of the wing. Squeaky sniffled and grabbed a tissue. Bill wiped his eyes with his sleeve.

"That was one of the most precious moments." He choked up, sitting down in his big leather chair. Squeaky knelt in front of him.

"Bill, you realize that you made all this happen for José."

"Oh, how's that?"

"Well, you left early this morning, flew to San Francisco, turned right around and came back, just to fulfill a little boy's Christmas wish." She laid her head onto his chest.

"He wanted to meet Steve Young, but the timing didn't

work with everybody's schedules."

"I know." She looked sweetly into his eyes.

"Anyway, I hope it gives José some hope."

"I'm sure it will. Hey, did I tell you yet today that you have such a kind heart?" Squeaky wrapped her arms around Bill's head as she stood. He ignored the throbbing pain from his bump. "You brought José's parents up from Mexico, employed them, then sponsored their immigration. Just so they could be close to José during his treatment."

"He would have been alone." He sniffled. "Little children just shouldn't have to go through certain things without their parents."

"Oh, Bill, just think. If José had not visited his aunt in Payson that day . . ." Squeaky stood to get the box of tissues.

"And had she not brought him into my office." Bill stood. Squeaky put a tissue in his hand. "It's been a two-way street, you know. José has treated me like his own grandpa." He blew his nose. Something felt like it popped in the bump. A surge of intense pain made his head pound all over. He squinted his eyes and clinched his jaw.

Squeaky handed him the waste basket. He reached out to take it. His hand missed it by half a foot. He stared at it, certain of its location. He missed it again and again.

"Bill, what's the matter?"

"I'm fine."

"You are not fine. Your pupils are uneven." She took him by the arm.

"I guess I bonked my head in the storm." He gazed forward, listing to one side.

"Bill?" Squeaky cried out.

"Angels, just like she said. Angels this Christmas." Bill took his Santa cap and beard off.

"Oh, my word, Bill! What in the world happened to your head?" She reached up and touched the bump. "You're head is swollen down to your neck. You need help, now."

Bill felt himself collapse into his chair. The room spun around him in a blur. He reached out to squeaky.

"Emergency?" He heard her call out in a panic. "Doctor! Nurse! Over here!" She stepped out into the middle of the ER. "It's Bill. Look at him. He's hurt and just passed out." Squeaky's voice faded out as darkness closed in around him.

Bill laid motionless in an isolated hospital bed. He sat in what felt like a soundless, lightless, and peopleless empty room. "Help," he called out. "Help me, somebody." His voice echoed back to him. He lingered ever so lonely and painfully here. His pain felt unbearable. It came from deep inside his chest and tortured him with an emptiness and nagging feeling of loss. He'd call out, but no one answered. No one ever attended his needs. The only constant he now could count on turned out to be what he came to refer to as the darkness.

Two

Lost in Room 1225

Four Years Later

BILL STARED out his window. He wore brown pajamas beneath an opened purple bathrobe. His leather sheep-skin slippers buffered his feet from the cold linoleum tiles on the hospital floor in room 1225 of Payson hospital's brain trauma wing. A CD player at the nurses' station just outside his room played a piano version of "White Christmas" that filled the hospital halls with sweet tones. Bill liked to listen to music. Every song he heard sounded brand new, every time he heard it. This day grew late. That frightened him. Sometimes, during the late hours, he suffered.

He kept looking outside his window as large snow flakes continued to cover everything. His window already had a foot of snow on its ledge. The glass looked matted by a nearly perfect oval of frost. Bill's attention focused on something much more interesting than the wintery scene on his window. He loved to watch the children as they played on the hospital grounds outside his window. His room overlooked the steep hill on the south side of the hospital that drew many thrill seekers to its long and steep slopes. He cheered each time a child sled down the hill.

"One-one-thousand, two-one-thousand, three-one-thousand, four . . ." He counted aloud how long it took for each child to sled from top to bottom. "Good run!" Bill exclaimed with a twinkling gleam in his eyes.

Two little girls reached the fence. They grabbed their sleds, then ran as fast as their little bundled legs would take them back up the long walkway leading to the south hospital doors. They ran past the statue of the Black Hawk Indian chief, past the first fountain, then past the second fountain. At the top of the lawn they rested to catch their breath. He waited patiently for them to sit down in their sleds and launch themselves again down the slopes. First one then the other slid, screaming all the way to the bottom.

The sun had set already. Only these two die-hard sledders remained. He did, too, hoping somehow they'd never want to leave. But then a minivan pull up to the bottom of the walkway. The girls dragged their sleds to the van, placed them up on the racks, and disappeared as the van turned the corner.

Bill desperately scanned for any other children he may have overlooked. He found none. He scanned it again, more frantically, looking left and right, back and forth. His hands trembled. "Please come back," he called out. "Where are the children?" He turned, fearfully scanning his hospital room. "The darkness comes when the children leave." He rarely remembered things, but he did remember the unbearable incarceration of the darkness. He folded his arms tightly, refusing to leave his post behind the window.

"Doctor Crandal, Doctor Crandal, you have a call on line one." A woman's voice announced over the PA system. Bill looked into the hallway to see a doctor as he walked behind the nurses' station. Bill pursued him, stopping directly in front of the nurse.

"I'm Bill." The music continued to play. She kept writing in her patient files. "Excuse me, I said I'm Bill. I'd like to meet the new doctor, Doctor Crandal." The nurse remained quiet. making no real attempt to look up at him. She stood up, then carried a file back to where the telephone sat on the desk behind the CD player.

She whispered to Doctor Crandal who nodded, said goodbye, then hung up the phone. He walked back with her.

"Oh, and Doctor Crandal, we have a new patient you should see," the nurse explained.

"No, I'm not new. I've always lived here," Bill pointed to himself.

"Really? A new patient this close to Christmas?" Doctor Crandal looked right past Bill into the room by the Christmas tree.

"He just arrived." She held up the patient chart. Doctor Crandal scanned it.

"Unfortunately, I don't have time right now. They've just called an unexpected board meeting up on the third floor. Seems the auditor is coming in to look at the books next week." Doctor Crandal kept looking past Bill. Bill turned around to see what might be so interesting to him back there. "I'll come back by after my meeting."

Bill turned back as Doctor Crandal walked away.

"You'll just have to wait." The nurse shrugged as she wrote something in the chart and laid it back down on the counter.

"I know," he mumbled. "I heard what he said."

Ring, ring.

"Hello, brain damage and recovery wing," the nurse answered. Bill eavesdropped shamelessly. "Yes. Oh, hello, Julie. Yes, I do remember. You called about your nephew this afternoon." The nurse looked up and stared at Bill. It made Bill feel self-conscious enough to reach down to his open robe, pull his right then left sides closed, then tie it around the waist. The nurse smiled briefly.

"I agree. He should have worn a helmet. No, I can't release his medical diagnosis to you. Only to immediate family. I tried to explain that to you before." She looked down at her watch. "I know you love him. But you will have to call your sister. She can tell you. Thank you, goodbye." She hung up the phone.

"I wish I had family," said Bill. "Then somebody would call to check up on my condition." He waited for the nurse to say something. She didn't, so he slowly walked back toward his room. She walked around her station and past him, entering his room first. At his bed, she quickly adjusted the blanket.

He went around her and the bed, returning to his post at the window. He didn't like his bed. He laid there each time the darkness came and held him captive for months on end. He hated going to sleep there.

"Dinner will be here in a few minutes," she said, walking around to the other side of the bed.

"I don't feel very hungry. I haven't felt hungry for a long time." He leaned onto the window sill to look for children.

"They made your favorite pudding."

"I just said I wasn't hungry," he growled.

"I'll make sure you get a special serving this time. Today is Thursday. Christmas Eve is in two days."

"I guess no one listens to me anymore." Bill turned around, but she'd stepped out into the hallway and on to another room. "I should have become a doctor. Then the nurses would pay attention to what I said." He glanced trough his door and down the hallway, noticing the plastic Christmas tree with its blinking lights, sparkling ornaments, and piles of presents.

"Trees with lights." He scratched the back of his head. "Must be some sort of celebration or something." He returned to his doorway. "Nurse, is there a holiday coming?" She ignored him, walking right past his door into the next room.

"Thanks for nothing." He eyed his bed. And she's not very good at making beds either. She left the blankets lumpy." He retreated back to the safety of his window again. He couldn't see much detail.

He waited and waited, arms folded tightly in front of his chest. Time meant nothing to him. Dinner came and went. He didn't eat one bite. The street light eventually turned off as the sun's light chased the night away. A few flurries fell here and there. Bill followed them with his eyes.

"I heard you like to look out the window." A female voice startled Bill.

"What?" Bill turned to see a beautiful young, twenty-something blonde. He looked her over. She wore white slacks, white shirt, white sweater, and white shoes.

"May I come in?" She politely asked.

"Sure, Cutie. What's your name?"

"Patricia. You can call me Pat though. I'm part of a new Christmas outreach program, here at the hospital. I'll be your community therapist."

"Oh, I don't need a therapist. I like looking out the window, so I'll just stay here," he said as he faced back toward the window.

"Really?" Pat walked over. "What's so interesting about snow?"

"I don't look at the snow. I like to watch the children that play in it," Bill felt nervous as he defended himself.

"I don't see any children out there." She looked past his shoulder.

"They come back in the day light. Wait here with me and you'll see them out there."

Just then, a snow plow pushed a massive wave of snow off the street onto a pile on the walkway that lead up to the hospital.

"Hey!" He waived his fist. "The kids can't get onto the grounds with that heap of snow in the way." The truck continued down the street.

"I heard you loved children."

"You heard?" He scowled. "Who's telling you things about me?" he complained, distracted by the plow.

"The same people who told me you had the most boring room in the entire hospital." They both looked around the room. "I mean, no pictures of family or friends, no art work, no decorations." Grey speckled white floor tiles covered the floor. A metal bed sat in the middle of the room with all kinds of gadgets, coming from all kinds of devices down to the bed. The tan blanket looked slept in. An old rocking chair sat next to the bed. It had a box and some paperwork on it.

"See what I mean?" Pat stared at the rocking chair for a minute.

"Yes, I do," Bill retorted. "I have no picture, because I'm alone. I have no art nor decorations because nobody ever listens to me. I ask for changes around here and they ignore me all the time." He faced the window but didn't really look out this time.

"You must really find that frustrating at times." She leaned a shoulder against the wall, searching for eye contact.

"Very. This is not a hospital room. It's a prison cell." He looked down. "But you listen to me."

"Well, it is Christmas. Besides, I heard you didn't like it here.

"Who would? This place is for people with brain problems." Pat clasped her hands together in front of her tummy.

"Who's got a brain problem?" He felt bothered. "Besides, I'm an unattached bachelor. I could be quite a catch for a young thing such as yourself." He raised his shoulders back and his chest out, turning for her inspection.

"You are very attractive, Bill, but I already have a man."

"Oh." His shoulders and chest slumped back down. He turned again to look out the window.

"Besides, I'm not here to court you. We've got work to do." She stepped away from the wall.

"Work?" His eyes opened wider.

"That's right. You're now part of a clinical experiment to see if rehabilitation comes through community outreach."

"Rehabilitation through what?"

"Through community outreach."

"What does all that mean?"

"It means we're going to get you better while we help others."

"I already know what gets me better. If the children come then the darkness stays away. So I stay here and look for the children." Bill felt threatened by the thought of leaving his window.

"Bill?" He knew she waited for him to look at her. He

didn't. "Bill, look at me." He looked. But not into her eyes. "Getting better means no more darkness, ever."

"Never?" He made eye contact.

"Never."

"But I'm afraid to leave the children. They need me to watch them. They make me better while I watch over them."

"They don't make you better. They just distract you. Wouldn't it be nice to feel safe and happy even when the children leave?"

"Yes. Can you do that? I mean can you help me feel happy and not so alone?"

"Not just me. You have to do your part."

"Really?" He put his finger to his chin as he pondered the idea.

"Yes, really. And others will help along the way, too."

"Will we work with the children who sled out there?"

"Let me think." She folded her arms and walked toward the door. "You know, the child we're going to help loves to sled. She and her parents are part of our first assignment." Pat smiled, nodding as she waited for him in the doorway.

"Our first assignment? I can't remember when I've been outside the hospital."

"I know. Hopefully, we'll fix that, too." Pat looked sincere. "It's okay, Bill," she whispered, extending her hand. "I've got approval from the highest level of authority. We can leave the hospital if we always stay together."

He walked past her extended hand into the hallway, not even caring that he still wore pajamas, slippers, and a robe. They walked as far as the hospital room next to the Christmas tree. Pat stepped inside. Bill looked in to find another young woman, a brunette, also dressed in white from head to toe, standing next to the patient's bed.

"Nadia," Pat called in a quiet voice.

"Hello, Pat," she said in a strong German accent. "I see you've met our Bill." She looked him over head to toe. "He's so adorable!" He raised his shoulders and chest again.

"We're heading out on our first assignment right now."

"I don't believe I've had the pleasure of making your acquaintance, Nadia. I'm from . . . I'm from . . ." He tried to remember. They stared at him, patiently waiting for him to finish. He struggled, looking back and forth at Pat and Nadia, and feeling embarrassed until he glanced back at his own hospital room. "Oh, yes, I'm from down the hall, room 1225." He announced proudly, sucking in his gut.

"Very, very, nice to meet you, Bill," she replied, pronouncing the r's more like w's.

Vewy. He wondered what that word meant as he smiled back.

"Bill, you and I have already talked a few times together."

"We have?" He slumped back down.

"Bill. Nadia and I will be working together with you. She's a memory recovery specialist." Pat explained reassuringly.

"Pat's right," Nadia explained, "but first, you and Pat need to get started on your first assignment."

"Then what?"

"Then we do other things, good things." Pat looked as if waiting for his reaction. He pondered quietly with his finger on his chin. "Does that sound acceptable?"

"I'd have to say it does. But can we watch the children sled first?"

"Maybe later. Can you wait 'til then?" Nadia shook her head.

"I guess, but I don't like it."

"Wonderful," Nadia replied.

Vunderful? he mused.

"I'll see you both later."

"Wait," he interjected. "who's in that bed, Nadia?" He pointed to a young man, whose head had been wrapped in a large gauze turban. Small blood stains soaked through the wrap. "He looks hurt."

"He is hurt, badly. I'm just doing my preliminary assessment. This is hard on his family, too," Nadia explained.

"Are you going to help him get better?"

"Yes." Pat and Nadia replied.

"Just not yet. Preparation must first be made." Nadia made a note. "Listen, Bill, I'll meet with you later. Best of luck on your first assignment." She continued to write on her clipboard and turned her back to Bill.

"Thanks, Nadia," Pat called back as they continued down the hall.

"What assignment did she mean, Pat?" Bill felt like a lost tourist, looking at everything as he followed behind her.

"You'll see. Let's get going." They traveled through town. Bill eventually stopped on the corner of Main and First Streets. "I'm confused, Pat." He shook his head.

"Why's that, Bill?"

"This looks so familiar, but then it doesn't at the same time. It's so frustrating to me."

"Bill, I know. Be patient, we're going to try to fix that."

They continued along as the snow fell gently. He didn't feel cold. In fact, he stuck out his tongue, trying to catch a snowflake. None ever landed on it. He saw light pole after light pole decorated with huge pine bow wreaths, holly berries, and red ribbons. Colorful lights hung between each pole, and signs that extended over the sidewalks read:

Happy Holidays
from
Payson's Historic District

"Pat, something important is happening here. Is it a holiday?" he explained with a concerned sound in his voice.

"Yes." Pat examined his expression. "What do you think it might be?"

"I don't know. Do you see that tree, decorated in front of that shop?"

"Yes, do you mean the big one in front of Roe's Bake Shop?"

"Is that a bakery?"

"Yes, it is."

"Oh, I'm not hungry now."

"Anyway, the holiday is called Christmas." Pat giggled. "It's morning and Christmas Eve is tomorrow night," Pat explained. Bill stared forward pensively. "You really do need my help, you know."

"Help with what, Pat?" Pat never answered. He soon forgot the question. They traveled on toward their first assignment.

☙ Three ❧

The Wilson Family Assignment

THE SUN topped the east mountain peak, casting its rays onto their backs. They stood on the sidewalk this quiet, wintery morning. Bill examined the snow covered, blue house. Red clay roofing tiles, emerged between patches of melted snow. This house, like so many other sites he'd seen this morning, looked very familiar in a distant, surreal way.

"This is one of Payson's older, historic homes," Pat explained.

"Really, how old is it?"

"Almost ninety years. When I was a little girl, I knew the people who built it."

"Oh?"

"Hey, you see that balcony up there?" She pointed to a balcony that covered the wooden porch below. The door leading onto the balcony had a widow's roost above it that stood about ten feet taller than the rectangular roof that spanned the house. Three dormer windows emerged from the roof.

"The builder's wife lived a very long time. In her later years, she'd sit on the balcony each evening, sewing and knitting as she watched the people pass by. They'd call up to her. She'd call and wave back"

"Sounds peaceful," said Bill.

"It was."

"Where is she now?"

"Moved on." Pat walked up to the end of the porch. He followed. "Now a small family lives here—a mommy, daddy, and a wonderful seven-year-old daughter, Shelly. I've been working with her for a while."

"Pat, I'm worried."

"About what?"

"Well, the string of Christmas lights on this house have icicles hanging off like they haven't been used. All the other houses lights are still on." Bill peeked into the front window. Everything inside looked dark behind the lace curtains.

"Very observant, Bill. These lights haven't been on for years. The family that lives here needs our help."

"They do?"

"We've got a great deal of work to do here," Pat sighed.

"I can't be much help, Pat." Bill folded his arms.

"Why would you say that?"

"People don't listen to me. They pretend that I'm not even there."

"Bill, don't you see yet?"

"What?"

"Haven't you ever heard that people don't care what you say until they know that you care?"

"I don't know." He scratched his head, trying to recall.

"The point is that they respond to our love just like everyone else in the world. It took many visits to get Shelly to listen to me."

"Oh?"

"You'll catch on soon."

Bill looked down at the deep snow under his feet. The porch laid under two feet of snow, except just in front of the door where it had been scraped back. Icicles hung three feet down from the balcony and a foot down from the lights. Bill reached out to touch one, but pulled his hand back when a young slender man, dressed in tan slacks, a maroon shirt, and a grey tie opened the front door.

His short brown hair parted from the left side in a meticulously combed style. He bent down to retrieve the morning paper and a quart of milk from the box on the porch. His breath fogged in front of his face as he eyed the headlines of his paper.

"He's a handsome young man," Pat whispered.

"He really is. Do I know him?" Bill whispered back. The young man looked away, then went inside, closing the screen and front doors. Bill and Pat quietly stood outside the front door.

"Shelly." Pat covered her mouth as she whispered.

"Who's Shelly?"

"Shh. Just pay attention." The front door opened to reveal a small little girl, holding her two fashion dolls. "Shelly, may we come in?" Shelly opened the screen door, scanning the porch. They came into the foyer as Shelly closed the doors. Bill looked around at the rest of the house. The living room sat to his right with a swinging door that had been propped open into the living room. The family room sat to his left. In the back corner of the family room stood a beautiful darkly stained oak spiral staircase.

"Have I ever been here before?"

"I can't say, Bill. Have you?" Pat waited for a reply.

"Maybe I could stay here. Is there a hill for sledding out back?"

"I don't think so."

"Oh, never mind then. . . . There's no tree or lights here, Pat."

"I know. They had a bad experience a few years ago."

Bill and Pat slowly entered the kitchen, trying not to make a big disturbance. The young man sat on one side of the table. He'd placed the milk bottle on the table. His wife and daughter sat across from him, but he didn't appear to notice them. Pat smiled and stood relaxed just inside the door. Bill stood anxiously next to her, examining the kitchen layout.

The hardwood floors looked original to the house. Behind the small round table, the kitchen counter sat with an opened box of shredded cereal, box of instant oatmeal, and loaf of wheat bread on it, nothing else. Pots and pans hung from the lattice work over the counter. The stove looked like the old time wood-fueled stoves, except it had modern knobs on its face. A large black pipe went from the back of the stove up and out at the top of the kitchen wall. Everything in here looked clean to Bill, almost unused. He kept waiting for something to happen at the table.

"Pat, something's wrong. It's too quiet." Bill had to lean down to whisper since Pat stood about a foot shorter than he.

"Shhh." Pat covered her lips with her finger. "These are the Wilsons. That's Nancy the mommy, Shelly the seven-year-old daughter, and Jacob the daddy."

"Does Shelly sled?" Bill noticed that Shelly looked at her dolls when he asked.

"Yes, now try to be quiet. Let's just listen," Pat whispered. No one at the table appeared to hear their conversation.

Bill studied Nancy, who sat at the table on Shelly's left. Nancy looked thin, very thin. She had short sandy blonde hair and wore sweat pants with a pullover sweatshirt that read *Payson Lions.* Jacob held the morning paper so high that he couldn't be seen as he read it.

"I received a Christmas card yesterday, Jacob." Nancy tried to start a conversation.

"That's nice. Did we send one back?" Jacob kept reading the newspaper.

"I guess not." Nancy picked up her spoon and poked at her shredded cereal and sliced bananas. She took the milk bottle and poured milk into her bowl, then returned the bottle quietly to the table. "I guess I'd have to buy them before I could send them, now wouldn't I?" Nancy scowled at the back of Jacob's newspaper.

"That's nice, Nancy." Jacob kept reading. Shelly silently sat back in her chair, her feet swinging back and forth about a foot above the floor. She held a blonde female fashion doll in one hand and a blonde male doll in the other. Her oatmeal sat untouched on the table in front of her. They all sat silent for a while.

"Shelly, does your Chrissy doll like your new Jim doll?" Jacob asked, barely glancing over the top of his newspaper.

"Mmmff," Shelly muttered without looking up at her dad.

"Chrissy doesn't like him?" Jacob looked at her, snapping his newspaper sharply as he turned the pages. Nancy and Shelly didn't even flinch. "Jim's not going to like being treated like that." Shelly kept looking at the dolls. Jacob kept waiting for Shelly to respond, but she didn't look up to him. He shrugged at Nancy, pursing his lips, and raising his right eyebrow. Nancy held her arms out in front of her as if to gesture innocence in the matter. Jacob retreated behind his newspaper again. Nancy shook her head, leaning forward with her face right in front of Shelly's.

"You're going to starve to death if you don't eat something, Shelly. Try to remember the other children in other countries who go hungry."

"Nancy, please don't give her that starving children speech again." Jacob implored impatiently. "It makes me feel guilty and I've heard it so many times that I now give to three international charities."

"You ignore me so much, how would you know how many times I give a speech?"

"Ignore you?"

"I'm only trying to help her, Jacob. Besides, I don't give the speech to you. I want Shelly to appreciate things and what they're worth."

"Then tell her about appreciating things, why don't you?"

"How would you know what I say when you're back there, hiding behind the newspaper all the time? You act like you live alone and there are two invisible people that live with you.

"Live alone . . ."

"Yes and another thing, you barely talk to me anymore."

"I'm just reading the morning paper."

Jacob and Nancy kept arguing. Shelly quietly walked out through the swinging door, unnoticed even though she kicked the swinging door shut. Bill and Pat followed Shelly between door swings.

"Chrissy likes Jim." Shelly snapped as the kitchen door

came to a stop. She sat back on a big green couch. Her feet hung over the cushion's edge. Bill and Pat walked through the living room, past Shelly, and over to the front door.

"What's going on?" Bill whispered, sounding concerned. "They barely said a word to each other, then suddenly there's this big argument."

"Lots of things are, Bill. That's why we're here on assignment—to help make things right again. These really are good people, they've just been through a great deal and it's worn them down." Pat looked back at Shelly, who groomed her dolls on the couch. "I know this may sound unusual, but for now we'll just talk to Shelly."

"That does sound unusual." Bill felt overwhelmed.

"Shelly will open up if we talk to her alone. She knows I love her and that helps her to hear me."

"So, when do we talk to her parents?"

"Once they feel your love, they open up their sensitivities."

"That's it. They just need to feel my love?"

"Well, I also find they listen better if I catch them apart. You saw what happened back in the kitchen. It's just difficult to get through to them when they're together." Pat started back into the living room.

"Pat, wait. What am I supposed to say?"

"Just say whatever you feel in your heart." Pat suggested as she sat down across from Shelly. Bill felt anxious as he sat down beside her. He watched Shelly comb her Chrissy doll's hair. Shelly wore pink pajamas with slippers sewn into the feet. When she looked up he noticed that her cute dimples. Her pretty blue eyes highlighted her blonde hair.

"Shelly?" Pat whispered in a nurturing voice. Shelly kept forcing the comb through her doll's long blonde hair. "Shelly, what's the matter?"

"Honey," Shelly pouted, still not looking up.

"Honey?" Pat leaned in a bit closer. Jacob slowly opened the swinging door until it rested again in the open position. They watched him walk through the living room and family room up the stairs. He didn't look at or say a word to any of them.

"I can't reach the honey," Shelly muttered, watching Jacob. "Mommy forgot to get the honey down and put it on my oatmeal. Doesn't she love me?" Shelly angrily directed the question to her Chrissy doll which she held in front of her.

"Shelly, I know your mommy," Pat calmly said. "She loves you very, very much. She and your daddy have been through a great deal of stress and heartache."

"I know!" Shelly rolled her eyes as she sat back further on the couch. "You don't have to keep telling me," she scolded the Chrissy doll.

"Let me just explain." Pat continued to speak calmly to her.

"I know!" Shelly insisted. "Daddy lost his mom and dad." Shelly placed the dolls beside her on the couch, sat back, and stared at the fireplace. "I just want some honey." She pouted with her bottom lip poking out.

"Wait here, you two." Pat got up and went back into the kitchen. Bill felt sorrow for Jacob's loss. The thought of losing his own mother and father felt unbearable to him. He wondered about his own parents. He must have had some. A few moments later, Pat returned and sat down beside him.

"Shelly." Pat waited for her to pick up the Chrissy doll.

"What?"

"I think your mommy will get the honey and milk in a few minutes."

"Thank you," Shelly whined.

"Did you notice that I have a friend with me today?" Pat gestured to Bill.

"Yes. Is he shy?" Shelly sat back up and held her Jim doll. Pat covered her mouth to hide her chuckle.

"I like to watch children sled," he blurted out.

"That's nice. What else?" Shelly patiently waited for him to reply.

"You have pretty eyes and pretty pajamas."

"You're funny," Shelly chuckled.

"Well, I just don't know what to say, Shelly," Bill whispered as he scratched his head.

"Don't worry, Pat taught me that it's okay to be a quiet person. She said the world needs at least some people to be quiet or else it could get real, real noisy." Shelly looked into the Jim doll's eyes. "You are a very handsome man."

"Are you talking to me?" Bill pointed to himself and looked at Shelly.

"Of course I'm talking to you, silly." Shelly smiled at the Jim doll. "Who else would I be talking to?"

"Oh, thank you. No one's ever called me handsome like that. I think."

"Well, you are. Isn't he, Pat?" Shelly arranged her Jim and Chrissy dolls face to face with their arms around each other in a hug.

"I guess he is." Pat blushed.

"She's very attractive, too. But she's taken. Some lucky guy beat me to her."

"Hm, uh," Pat cleared her throat. "Shelly, isn't today a half-day of school? The last school day before Christmas?"

"Yes." Shelly threw out her opened right hand. "And I don't know why. Teacher says we have to hold enough school days this year. But, I heard Mommy say that it's a waste of tax-payer's money."

Bill and Pat listened.

"I have to go to recess again." Shelly let her dolls fall to her lap as she dropped her head.

"The other children are so cruel to each other," Pat consoled.

"They hate me," Shelly pouted. "They make fun of me."

"I know what you mean. I saw it the other day while I watched you play."

"You came to my playground?" Shelly looked surprised.

"I stood right beside the fence."

"You can do that?"

"Bill and I can visit you anywhere, if you want."

"Will you come to the playground today?" Shelly waited

breathlessly for a reply. Pat looked to Bill who nodded.

"We most certainly will."

"Wahoo!" Shelly jumped up to her feet.

"Shelly," Nancy called from the kitchen. "I put some milk and honey on your oatmeal for you. Come and eat please."

"I've got to go eat my oatmeal." Shelly placed her two dolls into her back pack. "Bye."

"Goodbye." Bill stood up as Shelly ran back into the kitchen.

"Bye, Shelly." Pat stood and walked toward the front door.

"It must be time to go." Bill inquired, following Pat only inches away.

"Yes, it is."

"Pat?"

"Yes, Bill."

"Am I shy?"

"I don't know. Are you?" Just then, Jacob ran down the stairs adjusting his tie.

"Nancy, Shelly, I'm leaving." He opened the front door. No reply came from the kitchen while he finished with his tie. "Have a good day." Jacob murmured, walking through the door and not bothering to close it. Bill followed him out before the screen door closed.

"You have a good day, too, Jacob," Bill waved. Jacob glanced up to the porch, unplugged the extension cord from his engine warmer, and got into his big green SUV. "I think he wanted someone to say 'have a good day' back to him." Bill kept waving. Jacob backed out of the driveway and left for work. "Pat, he didn't wave back to me."

"That's is the hard part of this assignment,." Pat said through the screen door. "We're supposed to help, but people have to feel that we care. If they don't then they won't get it even when it's standing on their front porch."

"Pat, maybe we really can't help them."

"Why do you say that?"

"They don't talk to each other. The little girl only talks to her dolls, even with us sitting right in front of her. And the mommy and daddy fought." Bill folded his arms, looking back to her.

"I know." Pat's brow furrowed.

"Jacob." Nancy opened the screen door, walking barefooted onto the porch. Pat came out with her. "Jacob." Nancy looked at the empty spot in the driveway then covered her face with her hand.

"Jacob left for work, Nancy," Bill explained, but Nancy had gone inside. Pat stepped down to the sidewalk and waited for Bill to join her. He stared back at the door for a while.

"Bill, we need to check back in at the hospital before we go to Shelly's school for recess." A specialist is coming to see you." Pat extended her hand toward him. He continued to stare at the door.

"I don't want to go back. I like it here."

"This is where the family troubles are. Didn't you just complain about that?" Pat waited for his answer as he descended the steps and walked up to her. "What are you really afraid of back at the hospital?"

"The darkness. It traps me in the hospital on the bed."

"It won't while we're together."

"I guess that's true." He walked a few steps and then stopped.

"What's bothering you now?"

"I'm confused. I mean, I don't want the darkness and I can't figure out why you did this." He spoke sternly.

"Did what?"

"Why did you get me into the middle of this family mess? I can't help these people. They need a professional, not an invalid."

"Bill, you're not an invalid." She looked down as she turned to walk toward the street.

"That's another thing, Pat. You know too much about me. How did you get into my medical file?"

"I know too much about you, huh? Well, somebody has

to," she demanded as she waited by the mailbox. "Tell me something, Bill. Just why are you in the hospital's brain trauma wing? Tell me."

He scratched his head and tried to find the answer.

"Now then, how long have you been there? What did you do for a living before you checked in? What is your last name? Where's your family?" Her voice added pressure as it intensified.

"I can't really say." He stared blankly as fear filled his heart.

"You don't know, do you?"

He shook his head, feeling a pain from within his chest.

"We need to go."

"Please don't be mad. I like you, Pat."

"I'm not mad." Pat headed back to the hospital. Bill followed close on her heals. Neither said one word along the way.

Four

Memory Recovery Specialist

"THANK YOU, sir." Bill and Pat followed an elderly man through the large wooden doors on the north side of the hospital. The man ignored him. "I really care about you." Bill watched the man walk away. "Pat, I told him I cared. It didn't seem to matter." Bill folded his arms.

"Do you really care or did you just say that?"

"I think . . ." Bill thought about it. "I just said it, you know, so he'll listen."

"People need to know you really care. That's the key." Pat stood beside him, staring. He felt it.

"What?"

"Is something on your mind?" Pat inquired.

"Yes," he snapped.

"Would you tell me about it?"

"I don't want to talk about it."

"Well, would you tell me anyway? I am here to help you."

"Help me? In all my days, I never needed anyone's help. Why should I start needing it now?" Bill looked away.

"Step over here. You need to see something." Pat patiently led Bill to the west side of the ER where a large oak-framed full-length mirror hung. "Look in there. Who do you see?"

"I see a young woman who wants to become a do-gooder, but she's in over her head."

"Bill." Pat pointed to his reflection. "Could we just try to focus on you?"

Bill looked at himself. He stood lean and tall. He turned his face, revealing his young facial features—sharp jaw, masculine chin, and strong forehead. His flawless complexion highlighted his light blue eyes and sandy brown hair. "Aren't we both too young to be trying to save troubled families?"

"It's wisdom, not age, that matters. Besides, we're all the Wilson family has." Pat stood silently for a minute. "Bill, just how old are you?" Pat looked at Bill's reflection.

"Why, I'm . . . I'm . . ."

"You still don't know, do you?"

He shook his head.

"Look at yourself again."

He looked back at the mirror.

"Now, turn to the side."

He turned to his left.

"How old do you look to be, Bill?"

"I look . . . I guess the same age as you, twenty something."

"Now do you feel twenty something?"

"Not really. I feel about a hundred."

"Good."

"Good?"

"Yes. Part of what I want to do is to help you find out why you feel so old yet look so young." She turned him toward her. "Bill," she whispered, "you do need my help. Please let me help you."

"Help me with what?"

"How about with this question of your true age, for one thing."

"I don't know."

"Well, we don't have to make a decision right at this moment. Besides, the specialist is waiting for us. Look." They turned to see Nadia, standing alone beside one of the tables in the small cafeteria in the corner. She waved for them to join her.

"Who's that?"

"Your specialist. Remember? Her name is Nadia"

"I don't need a specialist."

"You'll just have to tell her that yourself." Pat walked away.

"I want to go back to my window," he said under his breath as he followed her across the lobby and into the empty cafeteria. The cafeteria looked more like a café. It had three small square tables, a microwave and three vending machines. They stopped across the table from Nadia, who silently looked up into Bill's eyes. He looked her over head to toe, pulling his chest and shoulders up again.

"Are you Nadia?"

"Why, yes. Do you remember me?"

"No. Pat said that was your name. But I don't believe we've had the pleasure of an introduction. You're quite the good looker. Perhaps we could go out, Nadia?"

"On a date?" Nadia glanced at Pat, who rolled her eyes and sat down at the table. "How very nice." Nadia's smile looked a bit strained. "I bet you and I do have a great deal in common. But I don't have time for a complicated relationship . . . the work and all." Nadia sat down next to Pat.

"Oh." He slumped back down, still standing behind his chair.

"You, Pat, and I have work to do."

"What is *vork*?" He innocently mimicked her strong accent.

"Work is, you know, tasks, assignments."

"Are you from Germany?"

"Not too far from Germany. I've come a long way to see you," Nadia offered. "You don't want to sit?"

"No, I don't."

"That's fine. I'm a specialist and you need my help," Nadia explained.

"I doubt that." Bill folded his arms. "Just what kind of specialist are you? I'm already under the careful attention of a very, very good physician," he proudly announced. "I can't think of his name. I do have a nurse, except she ignores me."

"Oh, I'm not a physician," said Nadia.

"You're not?"

"Oh, no. You don't need a physician at this point."

"I'm sure I do. I live in the hospital where children sled outside my window," he argued as he sat down.

"I've been a patient here for . . . for . . ." He felt stumped. His pompous anger quickly melted to confusion. Pat and Nadia watched him closely, anticipating the rest of his sentence. Bill wanted to finish his sentence, but his words disappeared in his mind before they could get off his tongue. He looked at them and began to tremble from the pain, coming full force from his chest. He buried his face in his hands and sat down, leaning both elbows on the table. "I can't remember."

"We know," said Nadia.

"Yes, we really can help you, here. But, we can't force you to take our help. You must choose to receive it."

"Will you let us help you?" Nadia and Pat stood together behind him, each with a comforting hand on his shoulder.

"Yes," he nodded, continuing to hide his face in his hands. He felt Pat and Nadia's gaze upon him. It felt safe to him. His pain began to lessen. He eventually looked at them.

"Thank you. Now, let's get started." Nadia and Pat sat back down.

"Nadia?" he whispered.

"Yes."

"I need to know what type of specialist you are." He waited for an answer.

"Bill, your doctor and nurse have done an excellent job for you. In fact they've done all they can at this point. I offer you a different service."

"What?"

"I'm a memory recovery specialist."

"I don't understand."

"It means that I am like an educator, a teacher. I teach people in your condition."

"You're a teacher?"

"Not in the classroom sense of a teacher. But, yes, I teach people one on one."

"What kind of students do you teach?"

"Well," Nadia leaned across the table, "your kind."

"What does that mean, my kind?"

"Good question." Nadia smiled. "That's where we will begin."

"Where?" He felt confused.

"Right at the question of what kind of person you are and I teach. I'd like to begin now, if you will allow it."

"Okay."

"Great, now this is your first test," said Nadia. "Just relax and do your best." He nodded. "Now, what is my name?" Nadia looked serious. Bill raised both eyebrows and tried not to smile.

"Well, that's an easy one. Your name is . . . is . . ." He struggled, closing his eyes and searching his mind desperately trying to find the name.

"What do you see inside your mind's eye?"

"It's the inside of a big empty building, like an airplane hangar."

"An airplane hangar? That's good. Let's use that. Do you see anything in the hangar?"

"Yes, just inside the door is a six-foot green tree."

"Is there anything hanging on it?"

"No. It appears to be just a tree. But it's scary in here like when I'm trapped in the darkness."

"It's okay. Pat and I are sitting here with you. There's no darkness."

"You'll stay with me?"

"Yes," they replied. This helped to calm his fears.

"Bill, look for a light of any kind."

"Come on brain," he muttered. "Come on. Wait, what's that?" He saw a flickering light in the back part of the hangar. He rushed toward it. It flew away from him. The more he chased it the further away it flew. "The light runs away from me."

"Let it come to you," Nadia instructed.

"I see it, there." He stood still in place this time. It moved toward him, shimmering and floating right in front of his face. He smiled. "It looks like a flying golden golf ball with light beams radiating out of its sides." He slowly extended his hand out toward it and it dropped down to his palm.

"I've got it. It's an ornament," Bill announced. "Wow!"

"What is it?" Pat asked.

"When I hung the ornament on the tree, about fifty other ornaments lit up all around its branches."

"Now, Bill, what is my name?"

"Nadia." He softly announced. "Your name is Nadia! And you're very cute." He opened his eyes.

"Why, thank you. You are cute, too." Nadia jotted a few things down on her clipboard. Pat smiled, eyes moist, covering her mouth with her hand.

"She's Nadia, the nurse," he announced proudly. Pat's face fell. Nadia put one finger over her mouth. Something didn't sound right.

"What's my name?"

"You're Nadia. But you're not a nurse. You teach kindergarten. No, wait a minute . . ." Bill closed his eyes and saw the hangar again. He searched for the ornament on the tree. "You are some sort of teacher, my teacher." He opened his eyes.

"And what is her name?"

"She's Pat. I know that one well," he replied immediately. Pat's looked appreciatively into his eyes. A peaceful confidence came into her face. This made him feel peace inside, too.

"You're doing fine. Just one last question for now. Why are you a patient in the hospital where children sled outside your window?" He closed his eyes for quite a while. Beyond the tree and its ornaments, the hangar sat dark. He shook his head.

"That's fine. You did wonderful, Bill. Pat, let's make another appointment for the three of us." Nadia stood and wrote on her clipboard. "We'll keep working with the hangar and Christmas tree image. It works exceptionally well for him. Oh, and

Pat congratulations. Your efforts with the Wilson family have already begun to show improvement in Bill's condition."

"I agree. Thank you," Pat replied.

"My pleasure. See you both later." Nadia walked out.

"Nadia the teacher," he stated proudly, watching Nadia walk away.

"Yes, good, Bill."

"Pat the therapist." He looked to Pat.

"Very, very good. Shall we go to Shelly's recess?" She walked out.

"Shelly? Recess?" Bill asked.

Five

Fat-Free Sugar-Free Hot Chocolate

PAT AND Bill stood inside the gate of the Barnett Elementary School playground. A thick layer of packed snow covered the entire play area. Nearly one hundred small children ran, climbed, and screamed as they played. Their loud and energetic voices made Bill smile. It reminded him of the noises from the children outside his hospital window. He noticed that one child sat alone on the swing.

"Look, Pat. Something's wrong with that little girl," he said, pointing.

"You found Shelly. Thanks." Pat walked on over to her and knelt down. Shelly sat quietly, holding her Jim and Chrissy doll.

"Shelly, how do you feel?" She tried to get Shelly to look up.

"Alone," Shelly pouted, her head bowed and her body curled over.

"Why are you so lonely, Shelly?" Bill knelt down beside Pat. "Look at all the young friends you have around here."

"Yes, they're having such a good time." Pat reached out to Shelly.

"They're not my friends," Shelly snapped at her Chrissy doll. "They all hate me and think I'm weird."

"I bet they don't think you're weird. Oh, dear, what happened to your eye?" Pat asked, covering her mouth with her hand.

"They did this to me." Shelly's lower lip quivered.

"That must have really hurt," Pat consoled.

"He said it was an accident."

"Who said that?" Bill demanded, climbing to his feet.

"That red-headed boy." She pointed to the merry-go-round. "He shut the door when I wasn't through it yet." Shelly shed a few more tears. "They all laughed at me."

"I'll go have a talk with him."

"No, that's not a good idea," Pat interrupted. "We can't talk to the other children here, just to Shelly."

"Really?" Bill and Shelly replied. He slowly knelt back down.

"Oh, yes," Pat said in motherly tone. "You are why we are here."

"Me?" Shelly whimpered, drying her tears with her mittens.

"Yes, you."

"Well, I'd give that little red-headed boy a talking to if he tried something again." Bill announced with an overstated bravado.

"Oh, don't, don't," Shelly insisted.

"No?"

"No, no. I'm sure he's really nice inside." Shelly held her Jim doll up closer to whisper in his ear. "You're nice, too."

"Uhhhmmf." He cleared his throat. Pat smiled.

"Children, children, it's time to come in for assembly," a teacher dressed in an elf costume announced from the steps. The children ignored her at first. "Children!" She put a hand on her hip and spoke sternly. This got some of them to start back toward the school.

"I've got to go to assembly." Shelly opened her backpack. "They make me keep you in here during class." Shelly started to put the dolls into her pack.

"Wait, Shelly. Can we see you later?" Pat inquired. "We want to talk to you about your parents."

"Can you walk me home? Please, I don't like to cross the streets alone," Shelly begged.

"We'll meet you out by the buses. Sound good to you?" Pat glanced up to Bill for his answer. He nodded.

Shelly nodded as she put the Chrissy doll away and ran off to join the mass of students entering the school.

"She's such a well-behaved little girl. Why is she so unhappy?" Bill scratched his head.

"That's part of how we can help." They stood beside the swing until Shelly entered the school. "You see, her daddy, Jacob has suffered great losses."

"What happened to him?"

"His mom unexpectedly got sick and died and then his dad, well, his dad's real bad."

"I couldn't bear those losses. He must be heart-broken," Bill lamented.

"He is. And the sad thing is that these losses have spilled over into their marriage. Jacob and Nancy live like strangers. They sleep in separate rooms, don't talk, and I fear they might separate if something doesn't change soon."

"Did you read their medical file, too?" Bill followed her.

"Yes. But, in a way I feel like I've known Jacob and Nancy their entire lives."

Downtown, they entered Roe's Bake Shop, walking past an assortment of pastries, doughnuts, cakes, pies, and rolls. Pat walked over to the corner booth. Bill sat across from her. The waitress stood with her back to them, wrapping utensils with paper napkins.

"I don't feel very hungry, Pat." He eyeballed the menu laying on the table.

"Me neither. Bill, I was so proud of you back at the playground when you showed Shelly you would stick up for her. You made her feel so important." Pat gently reached across the table and took both of his hands.

"Shelly is important isn't she?" He smiled, looking down at their hands.

"Yes, she's the key to our work with the Wilson family."

"Why is that? Why her and not her daddy? He's the one hurting so much."

"Because Shelly already listens to us and we don't have enough time to wait until Jacob listens that well."

"But she talks to her dolls."

"That's just her way of making sense of it all. She's really coping well. It's her parents who are ill."

"Hey," he said, "you're holding my hands. I thought you had a man already." She blushed, slowly pulling her hands away.

"I guess I do. I mean, of course I do." She sat back in the booth.

Ding-ding. Ding-ding. The bell on the top of the bakery door announced the entrance of two women.

"She looks familiar to me." Bill pointed. Pat turned around to see Nancy and another woman as they sat in the booth behind her.

"You're right, Bill." Pat whispered. "It's Nancy, Shelly's mommy."

He nodded.

"She didn't see us. Let's listen to what they talk about. Maybe it will give us some ideas." Pat motioned for him to move around the table and sit beside her. They eavesdropped over the top of the high-backed bench seat.

"We beat the crowds, Denise." Nancy placed her purse on the bench and loosened her scarf a bit.

"We always do. Hey, uh, are you and Jacob going anywhere tomorrow?" Denise asked.

"Probably not. Jacob doesn't want me, I mean doesn't want to go anywhere with me. We don't go places together much these days." Nancy motioned for the waitress to come over. An uneasy silence built up between Nancy and Denise.

"It's sad, you know?"

"What's sad?"

"You and Jacob."

"What are you saying?" Nancy sounded defensive.

"Oh, I don't know."

"What? Get it off your chest, Denise," Nancy semiseriously threatened.

"Okay, but don't get mad at me." She waited for Nancy to give a nod. "You and Jacob have always been the perfect couple. I was jealous when you met him, you know."

"No, I didn't know that."

"Not because he was good looking and not because he's a good breadwinner. I was jealous because there was something special—like a friendship that most of us never get to experience. You two were made for each other from the start."

"You think so?" Nancy sighed, reclining in the booth. She held her menu up, but didn't appear to read it.

"Yes, and I think you already know it." Denise gently took Nancy's menu and laid it on the table. "Admit it."

"I admit nothing."

"Admit it. You and Jacob were something special."

"Who cares what we once were anyway."

"I do," Denise replied.

"What can I get for you two today?" The young waitress held her note pad in anticipation.

"I'll take a fat-free sugar-free mint hot chocolate and a whole-wheat bagel," Nancy said.

"Would you like one of our flavored cream cheeses?"

Nancy handed the waitress her menu and looked to Denise. "No, thank you."

"And how about for you, ma'am?"

"I'll take a turkey croissant," Denise said, "with cream cheese." Denise emphasized the *cream cheese* part as she stared back at Nancy.

"Will there be anything to drink?"

"Yes, I'd like a fat-full sugar-full mint hot chocolate." She continued to stare.

"It'll be a few minutes." The waitress walked away. Nancy unwrapped her scarf and opened her overcoat. Denise kept staring and tapping her fingernail on the table.

"What is it now?"

"Nothing." Denise raised her eyebrows.

"Go ahead. Say it."

"It's just a little thing, really. But I guess since I'm your best friend I see things."

"What kind of things?" Nancy's voice revealed her irritation.

"Well, since you asked." She leaned forward across the table, excited to let it out. "Just that you stopped eating like a normal person about the time you and Jacob began to fall apart as a . . ." Denise stopped once she realized that Nancy looked wounded. "I'm sorry. I'll stop."

"You . . ." Nancy sniffled. "You are right. Jacob and I are in trouble. We . . . things . . . I . . ." Denise moved around the table and placed her arm around Nancy's shoulders.

"Listen, all couples have their rough times," she consoled as Nancy began to cry. "I'm here for you." She put her arm around Nancy's shoulders. Nancy took out a tissue and blew her nose. "You'll both get through this. I just know you will."

"I don't know. It may be too late."

"It's never too late, Nancy." Denise unwrapped her napkin from the utensils and handed it to Nancy.

"Thank you." Nancy blew her nose again, regaining her composure. "I just don't know what to do anymore. Everything I try seams to fail."

"Get it all out. I'm listening."

"That's it. That's all I have to say," said Denise.

"Well, I think you two just need something special." Denise gave Nancy another squeeze around the shoulders then pulled her arm away.

"Here are your orders." The waitress sat their food on the table. They began to eat without saying much else for a while. They ate silently throughout their lunch.

"I've got it!" Denise finished her last bite of sandwich.

"Got what?" Nancy finished off her chocolate. She placed ten dollars on the table.

"You and Jacob should go up to the winter cabin for Christmas Eve," Denise announced.

"Christmas Eve at the cabin?" Nancy blurted out, causing the waitress to glance at them. "Christmas Eve at the cabin. Are you mad?" she whispered.

"What's so mad about that?"

"That cabin belonged to Jacob's mom and dad. He's paid a caretaker to keep it up and hasn't gone near it since . . ."

"I know, dear, since he lost his mom." Denise wrapped her scarf around her neck. "That death was sad, Nancy. But what it did to you and Jacob as a couple is even more sad." Denise stood up and put on her overcoat, waiting for Nancy to finish putting her scarf around her neck. "It brought the demise of your friendship with Jacob." They walked out of the bakery. Pat and Bill faced forward.

"They have a cabin?"

"Yes, Jacob's mom and dad sold their Payson home on Goosenest Drive and moved into a cabin at the top of the mountain, above Payson Lakes. They used to live there year round," Pat's voice trailed off as though lost in her thoughts.

Bill waited patiently.

"I don't know why this didn't occur to me before."

"What?" Bill stared at her.

"Yes, I think the cabin might just be what we need."

"Why?" Bill asked as they exited the bakery and walked down the street.

"We have to get the Wilsons up to the cabin for Christmas Eve," said Pat.

"We do?"

"Yes, we do. Let's think about it while we go back to meet Shelly at her school."

"Sure."

"Isn't that someone we know?" He pointed to a green SUV as they crossed the busy street.

"Yes it is, Bill. That's Jacob, Nancy's husband," she replied. "Good for you. You've remembered Nancy and Jacob."

"I guess I did. How about that." He beamed.

"Now what's Jacob doing at the South Valley Realty office? I hope the Wilsons aren't going to move from that beautiful home they remodeled," Pat wondered aloud.

Bill shrugged his shoulders as they crossed the street, hurrying to get back to Barnett Elementary.

❧ Six ❧

Christmas Photo Album

PAT AND Bill stood in front of the school busses. The children poured out of the school, running and rejoicing as the bus monitor at the front doors of the school tried in vain to get them to walk. Each had a Santa Claus badge that looked handmade out of red and white construction paper and cotton balls. Each also had a large candy cane. Bill smiled, soaking in their energetic joy. The crowd soon shrank.

"Look." Bill pointed up the sidewalk. "Isn't that her?"

"It is." Pat explained as they hurried to catch up to her. "Shelly," Pat called. "We were waiting for you by the busses as we promised." Shelly took her two dolls out of her backpack and put the candy cane in their place.

"I didn't see you. I figured you didn't come," Shelly scolded her doll.

"We wanted to come see you," Bill added.

"Mommy used to walk me home but not anymore."

"Shelly, do you like stories? I'd like to tell you one." Pat waited for Shelly's reply.

"Oh, yes." She smiled at her Chrissy doll.

"Well, once upon a time . . ."

"Oh, goody!" Shelly hugged her two dolls.

" . . . there was a beautiful little girl. She had blonde hair. About as long as yours."

"Really, did she go to school?"

"Oh no, Shelly, she was too young for school. She was just a little, little, girl in this story. Not a big girl like you."

"Yeah," Shelly agreed.

"Anyway, this little girl was beautiful . . ."

"Did she have a pony tail? I did when I was a little girl."

"Oh, yes she had a pony tail, Shelly. And she loved winter time. Do you know why?"

"Why?"

"Because winter meant Christmas time would soon come. And this little girl's family had a big Christmas every year," Pat whispered as though she shared a top secret.

"They did?" Shelly whispered back. Bill acted as crossing guard, still listening to every word.

"This little girl woke up one morning and discovered that she, her mommy and daddy, and grandmom and granddad were all going to spend Christmas near Payson Lakes in a cabin!"

"That sounds wonderful!" Bill exclaimed.

"It does, it does!" Shelly added, stopping on the sidewalk and holding her dolls in front of her. "I'd love to go to a cabin in the mountains for Christmas."

"I bet you would. Anyway, they all drank hot chocolate, decorated the cabin . . ."

"Did they sled?" Bill asked with a childlike enthusiasm.

"Yes, they sled and sled and sled some more."

"Wow!" Shelly and Bill both exclaimed.

"Yes, and they had wonderful desserts and lots of food, and on Christmas Eve . . ." Pat paused her story to build the drama.

"Yes, yes . . ." Shelly begged.

"Granddad told the most wonderful Christmas story that everyone loved to hear." Pat finished. She and Bill stopped in front of the Wilson's home. Shelly beamed with excitement.

"Could I go to the cabin for Christmas?" Shelly asked her dolls. Bill and Pat glanced wide-eyed at one another.

"Oh, I don't know," Pat answered as they approached Shelly's porch. "What would your parents say?"

"They can come, too!" Shelly announced.

"I think it's a wonderful idea, Shelly. You must ask your mommy and daddy first."

"I will!" Shelly ran toward the porch then stopped in the snow. "Wait, who's the little girl? Who do I ask?"

"Yeah?" Bill added.

"Oh, you know them. Your mommy and daddy have pictures of them and the cabin in their Christmas photo album."

"Wahoo!" Shelly jumped up and down.

"You'll have to find the photo album without your mother's help. Let it be a surprise." Shelly nodded, still smiling big. "We'll come see you later." Shelly opened the screen door. Because she had two dolls in her hands and because her mittens slipped repeatedly on the cold door knob, she struggled to get it open.

"Hello, Shelly," Nancy greeted, opening the door.

"Pat?"

"Yes, Bill."

"That was a wonderful story. I wish it were true." Bill watched Pat slowly turn away, walking quickly back the way they'd came. He followed a few steps behind.

"It's not made up. It's a true story."

"Really?" He caught up to her. "Who owns a cabin up by Payson Lakes?"

"You . . ." Pat's head snapped quickly toward him, her voice strained by her frustration. "You don't remember the conversation we overheard at the bakery?" Bill looked down at the snow-packed sidewalk as he took a few more steps.

"What bakery?" Bill asked with a furrowed brow and a frown. "Please don't be mad."

"I'm not mad," Pat comforted as they walked back to the realty office a few blocks away.

"Pat, can you slow a bit?"

"No, please just keep up. We need to find out what Jacob is up to at the realty office."

❧ ☙

They followed another customer into the office and patiently waited behind him as he talked to the receptionist. Bill didn't like this place. It's cinder-block walls, linoleum floors, and old furnishings felt cold and reminded him of the hospital.

"Well, that's the long version of the story, Norm," Jacob said loud enough that Bill and Pat overheard him from the foyer. They walked toward Jacob's voice into a large room with numerous portable walls which connected a labyrinth of cubicles.

"You're right, Jacob. Lots of serious things have been happening in your life. So how can I help you today?" Jacob leaned forward across Norm's metal desk and laid a large photo album upon it. The album looked worn. Its brown leather cover had faded around the edges and along the spine. It had an inlaid Christmas tree on the front cover and read

Wilson Family Christmas Album

Jacob opened it. Pat and Bill went into the next cubicle to eavesdrop. Norm stared at the album while leaning back in his chair. He chewed on his pencil, as though anxious about something.

"Let's just listen quietly to what they say," Pat whispered. Bill nodded.

"I have this cabin. It's the one in that picture there," Jacob explained.

"Do you live there?"

"Not really."

"Not really?"

"No." Jacob shook his head.

"Well, I have to wonder what condition it's in."

"I've kept it maintained. I called Charlie, the caretaker last week and had him do a deep cleaning in case we, you know . . ." Jacob looked torn to say what he tried to say. "you know . . ." Norm leaned in a bit, waiting for the rest of the sentence. ". . . showed it for selling or something like that." Jacob's voice trailed off.

"You've had a caretaker?'

"Yeah, Charlie's an old friend of the family. He lives in his own cabin not far away."

"I see." Norm looked back and forth between the photo and Jacob. "Jacob," he inhaled deeply, "do you really want to sell it?" Norm asked. Jacob looked down at his knees. He didn't reply, just sat pondering. "I asked, did you want to sell it?"

"I think so," Jacob replied, unconvincingly. Pat covered her mouth. Norm removed the photo and examined it as he leaned back into his chair.

"You don't sound sure. Isn't it your cabin?"

"Well, mostly."

"Mostly?" Norm sat back up. "I can't sell a cabin that is mostly owned, Jacob."

"Let me explain. Mom and Dad lived in this cabin for a few years. They designed it, built it, and it was their home up until Mom passed."

"I'm sorry, Jacob. I heard about that."

"It's been a few years."

"And your dad?"

"I lost him."

"He passed, too?"

"No, but it has the same effect. He's got Alzheimer's and some other complications. It started shortly after Mom's passing. I don't know how he's hung on this long." Jacob stared past Norm, lost in his own thoughts and feelings. Norm nervously examined the picture of the cabin a few times.

"Jacob, I can go up, look at the cabin, get an appraiser to go up the cabin with me."

"What? I'm sorry. What did you just say?"

"I was just saying . . ." Norm stood up. "Let me keep this picture. It's Christmas Eve tomorrow." Norm cleared his throat. "And everybody's gone until next week."

"I see." Jacob stood. "That's a good idea."

"Yes, and we can talk after your dad has . . . I mean after the holiday."

"Sure, Norm. We'll talk then." Jacob followed Norm as they walked out.

"Jacob," Bill called. Jacob stopped. "Don't forget the photo album." Jacob turned toward the desk, retrieved the album, then left.

"Whew! Quick thinking." Pat said.

"What do you mean?"

"Well, I mean you reminded Jacob about the album."

"I guess I did." He smiled confidently. They walked outside, across the street, and up toward the hospital.

"The important thing is that Jacob heard you. He's feeling your caring influence."

"I hadn't thought of it."

"You're a good man, Bill."

"I am?"

"Yes, you just don't know it."

"Is that a compliment?"

"Yes. We need to hurry. I forgot that the specialist is meeting us again." They hurried up the long walkway past the statue and the two fountains to the south entrance of the hospital. Pat stood under the red stone arch. Bill stopped at the fountain, watching the many children sled down the hill.

"Bill, come on." Bill felt reluctant to go on in to see the specialist. He'd rather watch the children.

"Please, Bill." Pat persuaded him. He put both hands in his pocket with a sad expression on his face as he walked up to the doors.

"What's the matter?" she asked as he arrived under the arch.

"I just like to watch the children."

"Are you afraid of the darkness still?"

"Yes!" He snapped back, clinching his jaw. "It's always here and it's so strong."

"When is the last time it took you?"

"I don't know. It can take you when you're away from the children." He felt such a deep internal pain at the thought of the darkness. "Don't you see the danger, Pat?"

"Yes, I do. The darkness is not to be taken lightly. Try to remember that you and I have been away from the children for a long time. And no darkness"

"That's true." He felt the tension leave again.

"Someday, you may not have to worry about the darkness."

"That's right. I forgot. So what do I have to do next?"

"Let's meet with Nadia right now."

They entered the large double wooden doors to find Nadia waiting inside. He recognized the busy hospital sounds—phones ringing, people talking, and footsteps coming and going from many different directions across the hardwood floors.

"Sorry, Nadia," said Pat.

"Don't worry about it. Can we meet down in the Cowboy Room this time?" Nadia motioned for them to join her. They descended the short flight of stairs and turned left into an office area where desks lined the walls. A small round table with four chairs sat in the middle of the room.

Dedicated to the cowboy in all of us. Bill read from a plaque on the wall next to the doorway. They all sat down at the round table. Paintings, depicting western cowboy scenes, covered the walls above the desks. Bill recognized something about this room. He sat down with the others, lost in his search for what that might be.

"Bill?" Nadia glanced up from her clipboard.

"We're in the Cowboy Room," he calmly announced. Both Nadia and Pat looked surprised by what he said. He felt nervous because of their reaction.

"How did you know that? Did you remember?" Pat reached out across the table, stopping short of touching his hand.

"No, it's on the plaque by the door." He pointed back to the door. Their expressions fell.

"Good for you for reading the plaque then," Pat said, forcing a smile.

"What is the Cowboy Room, Pat?"

"It's a left-over from when this building served as a museum. This was the cowboy exhibit."

"Oh, nice room, huh?" He looked around at the wall hangings.

"Who am I?" Nadia leaned back, waiting for an answer.

"You're Nadia. And I bet you're very happy."

"Why do you say that?"

"Well, because you are a teacher and you get a few weeks off for the holidays."

"I do?" Nadia raised both eyebrows.

"Wait a minute. You don't teach school." He scratched his head. "You teach me."

"You remembered. Very good." Nadia made a quick note on the clipboard. "You are making progress. I have another question for you."

"Shoot, Nadia." He made pistol gestures with both hands.

"Have we met like this before?"

"Well, I can't really say."

"Bill, sit back, close your eyes, and search for the hangar in your mind's eye again."

"All right," Bill began to relax his breathing. He saw the same large hangar and Christmas tree. "I see it, but nothing's coming back to me."

"Wait, let me ask another question." He opened his eyes to look at her. "What did you and Pat do just before you came back to the center?"

"Oh, that's easy. We just . . . just . . ."

"Take your time on this one," Nadia gently instructed.

He searched the hangar in his mind.

"Try this approach. Do you see the Christmas tree with the glowing ornaments?"

"Yes, it's right there."

"Good. Now is there a small, colored light bulb anywhere?"

"Here, on the floor, a red one about an inch long."

"Pick it up and look on the tree for a string of lights. Got it?"

"Yes, there it is."

"Good, now put the bulb in the empty socket.

"Wow!"

"What?"

"It lit up hundreds of colored lights around the tree. Hey, and a small part of the hangar behind me just lit up, too."

"Describe it to us."

"It an older building on a busy street. It's the South Valley Realty office," he announced. "We were watching Jacob and the realtor guy, Norm." He opened his eyes and looked at Nadia. She and Pat both had leaned forward with their elbows on the table and their hands clasped together.

"You're right," Nadia announced.

"I guess I am."

"This has been the most successful appointment. I have to leave now. Sorry, I have a very busy work schedule. Let's meet again." Nadia rose to her feet, placing the clipboard under her arm.

"Wonderful. Just wonderful," Pat joyfully exclaimed.

"What?" he inquired.

"You're showing steady improvements. You're recovering," said Pat.

"How?"

"Well, you are helping with the Wilsons. That's bringing your ability to remember back to you." Pat added as she followed Nadia through the door and up the stairs.

"Nancy, Jacob, and Shelly?"

"Yes, Bill. The Wilsons," she replied. Nadia exited out the double wooden doors. They waived goodbye to her.

"How?"

"It's kind of complicated, but I promise you'll see the answer soon." They ascended the stairs into the main lobby of the ER. Bill smelled the medicinal smell of the ER. He couldn't tell exactly why, but he knew he didn't like ERs. They stopped on the west side. A woman with tear-soaked eyes, holding a tissue over her mouth, walked out of the doctor's office, past them, and on into the brain trauma wing.

"Oh my."

"What, Pat?"

"She just found out the diagnosis." They followed the sad woman until they stood outside the door of the room next to the Christmas tree. They saw the woman collapse across the listless body of the young man with the gauze turban.

"My son," she wept, holding him. He didn't hold her back. He laid there motionless, head bandaged, air tube in his mouth, wires connected to his body. Soon the woman walked over to shut the door, leaving Bill and Pat in the hallway.

Ben Richards, Bill read the name on a slip of paper taped to the door.

"Do you work with them, too, Pat?"

"No. The Richards case is a special one. I heard it will take two community therapists for this family and they're not quite ready for help yet." Pat lowered her head and leaned on the door jamb.

"What's the matter?"

"I guess . . ." Pat sighed. "I guess I'm just not used to seeing a mother who just heard a sad prognosis about her brain-dead son. It weighs my faith down."

"Haven't you done a lot of Christmas outreach therapy?"

"No, you are my first patient. The Wilsons are my first assignment." Pat walked down the hall.

"Only your first?" He followed a few steps behind. "Pat," he called out. She stopped. Bill hurried past her to see her face. She looked down. "You're doing a good job with me," said Bill.

Her stern expression melted away.

"I mean, for your first time and everything."

"That is very kind. Thank You." She glanced into his eyes then walked on.

"What's next?" he called.

"Next, well, we have to get up to the Wilson's house again."

"What for?"

"Breakfast."

"Oh, I'm not really hungry."

"I know. But, we still need to get the Wilsons to go up to the cabin for Christmas Eve. While we worked with Nadia, the sun set and rose again," Pat explained.

"It did?" He looked out the large plate glass windows. "I didn't even notice."

"Well, it's the morning of Christmas Eve. Hopefully the Wilsons will sleep in their cabin tonight." She worried aloud as they left.

"They have a cabin?"

Pat looked down, shaking her head.

"Just kidding, Pat."

"What did you just say?" She said as she whipped around toward him. "What did you just say?"

"Jacob was talking to Norm about selling it. Wasn't he?" Bill grinned.

"Bill!" Pat raised both eyebrows. "You just told a joke."

"I did," he beamed.

"Well, I'll have to let Nadia know at our next appointment. That's the first joke you've told since . . ."

"Since when, Pat?"

"Well, for years anyway. Congratulations, Bill. You really are making progress."

"Yeah."

"Let's get ready for breakfast with the Wilsons?"

"Let's get ready."

They walked on up the sidewalk.

Seven

Sausage, Pancakes, and Syrup

BILL AND Pat waited on the end of the front porch. The sun rose again over the east mountain peak. The clouds cleared out and the wind stopped, leaving a bitter cold behind. They didn't care. They stood certain in their resolve about the Wilsons going up to the cabin. Jacob came out of the front door on to the porch—leather slippers, pajamas, and an opened robe. He reached down to get the paper, flipping it open.

"Oh, no. Santa's sleigh may have mechanical problems. Will he make it in time for the children?" He read the headlines out loud. Pat and Bill walked up and stood quietly behind Jacob's newspaper.

"Did somebody open the front door?" Nancy yelled from inside. "I feel a draft."

Jacob turned, tugging on the left and right sides of his robe to close it. He reached down to retrieve a quart of fresh milk from the dairy box then walked into the house. He shivered as he closed the door.

"Shelly," Bill and Pat called. The front door opened. Shelly stood in her pink pajamas. She rubbed her eyes with the knuckles of one hand and held her two dolls in the other. She opened the screen door for Pat and Bill to enter, not looking up.

"Thank you." Pat and Bill hurried in.

"Shelly, would you and your friends shut the front door all the way, please?" Nancy called from the kitchen.

"Hey." Shelly looked sad as she closed the doors.

"Hey, are you still sleepy?" Pat asked.

"No."

They followed her into the living room, where she sat on the couch. Something felt different in the house this time. Bill glanced into the kitchen.

"Shelly, how did everything go here last night?"

"I got in trouble."

"For what?" Bill asked. "I hope it wasn't because of the bruise under your eye."

"No, my mommy called teacher and teacher got into trouble for that," she sighed.

"Then what, Shelly?" Pat patiently inquired above the noises of food preparation, coming from the kitchen.

"I guess I made a big mess upstairs."

"Oh, I see. You were looking for the photo album, huh?" Pat consoled. Shelly nodded with a gentle pout.

"Shelly, come to breakfast." Nancy called from the kitchen.

"I gotta go."

"And Shelly, leave your dolls on the couch." Jacob ordered.

"Uh, oh." Shelly muttered, placing Chrissy and Jim on the couch.

"It will be fine," Pat suggested as they followed Shelly into the kitchen. Shelly sat down in her regular seat. Bill and Pat stood in the doorway.

"Some days, I like to have breakfast with just the three of us." Jacob looked at Shelly then laid his newspaper down on the table. Nancy sat up straight. "Nancy, shall we have the usual this morning?"

"Well, not exactly" Nancy stood, eyeing Jacob. "Since this is the morning of Christmas Eve, I made a special breakfast."

"You did?" Shelly and Jacob sounded surprised.

"I did," Nancy replied in a monotone voice. She walked over to the stove.

"No oatmeal today?" Shelly asked.

"No."

"No whole wheat toast for me?" Jacob turned to watch her.

"No toast." Nancy returned with a frying pan. "And no whole shredded wheat cereal for me." She removed the lid to reveal sizzling sausage and steaming scrambled eggs.

"Wohoo!" Shelly exclaimed. Nancy served large portions to Jacob and Shelly. She also put a very small portion on her own plate.

"Nancy, this is a great idea." Jacob placed his napkin onto his lap.

"Well, I'm glad you both like it, because I also made buckwheat pancakes to go with it."

"You did?" Shelly and Jacob replied.

"I did." Nancy returned from the stove with a large stack of pancakes and put some on Shelly's and Jacob's plates.

"Mommy, can I have syrup?"

"Yes, you may." A look of both concern and excitement crossed Nancy's face. Bill didn't understand it all. She put half a pancake onto her own plate. Jacob poured syrup on his pancakes then handed the bottle to Shelly. Shelly and Jacob dove into their breakfasts.

"This is so good," Jacob spoke with his mouthful. "Nancy, aren't you going to splurge with us?" Nancy looked down at her half sausage link, small serving of eggs, and remaining small bite of pancake.

"Believe me, I am splurging," Nancy said, defending herself. "This isn't easy for me." She looked wounded. Her eyes expressed a vulnerability, which appeared to soften Jacob's expression.

"I don't really understand, Nancy. But I'm okay about it."

"Thank you, Jacob."

"Uh oh, sorry." Shelly spilled some syrup onto her pajamas.

"Be careful, Shelly," Nancy urged. "That's a special syrup."

"I can clean it up myself." Shelly jumped down to the floor and walked out into the living room. Pat followed right behind her. Bill stayed put. Shelly soon returned with a wet washcloth. She cleaned her spill from the table top then sat back down.

"That's very good, Shelly," said Nancy. Jacob didn't notice. He kept eating.

"Daddy, I've been very sad lately," Shelly announced. Nancy raised her eyebrows.

"We've noticed, Shelly. Why?" Jacob leaned closer to her, sipping water from his glass.

"Well, there's this little girl with blonde hair and a long pony tail and she gets to go to a cabin up at Payson lakes every Christmas."

Jacob's jaw fell open, nearly dropping a mouthful of sausage onto his plate.

"Daddy, you . . ." Shelly pointed to Jacob's mouth and back to her own. "Your food is falling down."

"Sorry." Jacob chewed a few more times and swallowed hard.

"I'm sorry, too, Mommy." Shelly turned to Nancy. "I made a mess yesterday, trying to find the photo album with the pictures of the little girl and the cabin."

"Did you find it?"

"No." Shelly put an oversized bite of pancake into her little mouth. Syrup ran down her chin.

Jacob froze. His eyes moistened. Nancy reached across the table to him. He looked like a broken-hearted little boy. Bill felt an urge to reach out to him in some way. A single tear rolled down Jacob's cheek and hung to the edge of his chin. He placed his napkin on the table and quietly left the kitchen. Nancy's hand remained extended toward Jacob's empty seat.

"Why's Daddy crying?"

"Lots of reasons." Nancy slowly drew her hand back as she wiped her eyes with her napkin. "It's not your fault." She pushed her plate away.

"Pat, what can we do?" Bill yearned for some way to help them.

"Shhh, just wait," Pat whispered, motioning for him to stay put. Jacob returned to his chair. He sat quietly for a while, looking back and forth at them. Bill felt the build-up of tension. He braced himself for what he thought would certainly be another big argument.

Thump! Jacob hoisted the photo album beside his plate on the table. Shelly and Nancy jolted.

"How did you find that?" Nancy asked. " I hid that under the bed."

"I looked under the bed, Mommy. I didn't see it."

"I had it with me. I showed it to Norm."

"Norm, the realtor?" Nancy frowned.

"Yes, but nothing happened. I mean, I couldn't. I wanted to. But I just couldn't." Jacob opened up the photo album and turned a few pages. "This, Shelly, is the beautiful little blonde-headed, pony-tailed girl you spoke of."

"She's pretty, Daddy."

"She's still pretty, Shelly." Nancy looked back and forth between Shelly and the picture.

"She is? I'd like to meet her." Shelly held the fork with a very big piece of pancake in front of her face. The syrup dripped down to the table top. "What's her name?"

"Shelly," Nancy replied. Shelly laid her fork down on her plate.

"This is you, Shelly. You're sitting in Grandma's lap." Jacob's voice broke.

"I have a grandma?"

"Yes, you do." Nancy put her hand on Shelly's.

"I want to meet her. I want to sit in her lap again." Shelly begged. Jacob turned half-way toward the stove. Bill reached out and put his arm on Pat's trembling shoulder.

"I want you to sit in her lap, too," Jacob said, "but Grandma died." Tears rolled down both cheeks.

"She did?" Shelly whispered. "Grandma must be your mommy, huh?"

"Yes, she is."

"Did Grandma die forever?" Shelly asked. Jacob didn't answer.

"She didn't die forever, Shelly. Someday we'll see her again."

"In heaven?"

"Yes, Shelly, in heaven," Nancy replied.

"Is that my Grandpa? Is he dead, too?" Shelly whispered. Jacob drew his head back, looking at the ceiling.

"Maybe we should close the photo album for now." Nancy reached out to take it.

"No, please." Jacob shook his head. "I can't run from it anymore." Jacob stood and walked over to the counter, leaning heavily upon both arms. Nancy followed him but stayed a few feet back. "I can't hide any more!"

"Oh, Jacob." Nancy wrapped both arms around his waist. "I do love you." Jacob placed his arms onto Nancy's.

"I love you, too," he whispered.

"Ask them now," Pat called out from the door. Shelly walked over and stood behind her parents.

"Mommy, Daddy, could we go here for Christmas Eve?" Shelly held up the photo. She pointed to a picture of the cabin. "Let's go to the cabin and tell stories and drink hot chocolate."

"Oh, that would never work." Nancy shook her head slowly. "I'd have to rush with Shelly to get supplies from the store."

"And I can't shake the feeling that I need to talk to Dad in the hospital." Jacob stared at the two of them.

"Do, Jacob. I think it will be good for you." Nancy put her arm around his back.

"Nancy, Shelly," Christmas will be rough this year. Because we are going up to the cabin at Payson Lakes."

"Wahoo!" Shelly leaped into Jacob's arms, her little feet dangling.

"Is that all right with you, Nancy?"

"Absolutely! Oh, my!" Nancy said.

"What?" Jacob asked.

"It's the morning of Christmas Eve and I haven't bought a single Christmas present. I feel so ashamed." Nancy clinched her jaw.

"So what! Let's not buy any presents this year. Let's just be there for each other, together up at the cabin." Jacob lowered Shelly to the floor. Nancy bit her fingernail as she looked to Jacob then to Shelly.

"How do you feel about it, Shelly? I mean if we had no presents at all?" Nancy asked.

"Wahoo!" Shelly screamed, raising both hands above her head. "We're going to the Christmas cabin! Wahoo!"

"All right, all right then." Nancy smiled. Jacob kissed her on her cheek. She touched her cheek, staring into his eyes. He smiled. Shelly walked over to the swinging door.

"Excuse me, people. We've got a cabin trip here. No time for the mushy stuff." Shelly instructed in a falsetto voice.

"Wait, if we're going to the cabin today, we'd better have Charlie get things cleaned up. Do you think he can with this late of notice?" asked Nancy.

"I'll call him and let him know our new plans. I'll also drop you two at the grocery store and I'll go over to the hospital.

They left the breakfast mess, quickly got dressed, and drove off in their green SUV. Pat and Bill went directly to the hospital and waited for Jacob in the brain trauma wing.

Jacob eventually walked to the doorway of his dad's room.

"Bill, you go in alone with him."

"Me? Come with me, Pat." Bill worried about how he could help.

"No. He already listens to you."

"Pat, you know so many things. I'm . . . I'm kind of clueless." Bill lowered his head.

"Bill, it's not what you know or don't know."

"Oh?" Bill looked up to Jacob.

"You see, Jacob needs a fatherly figure. You're best suited for that, not me."

"But what if I mess things up?"

"Then we'll just have to fix things again. Now go. I'll wait in the ER for you." Pat walked away. Jacob stood in the open doorway as though a force field blocked his entry. Bill stood beside him.

Eight

Jacob and His Dad

"JACOB." A middle-aged nurse came up to the door.

"Hey." Jacob turned but didn't look up at her.

"Are you here to see your dad?" She clasped her hands. Jacob nodded. "I'm glad you came today."

"Why's that?"

"Jacob, we were going to call you. Your dad's test results just came in. His kidneys are failing. In fact, it's just a miracle that he's alive at all."

"I was afraid of that." Jacob finally glanced at her.

"Jacob, I've known your dad for a very long time. I admired his work for many years."

"Thank you."

"He's a fine man. I just needed to tell you that." She extended her hand. Jacob reached out and shook it. She walked away.

Bill remained silent.

Jacob took a deep breath and held it. He slowly stepped into the room, closed the door, and walked in, stopping next to his dad's bed before he released his breath. Jacob looked pitifully at his dad who laid motionless under the hospital blanket. Bill stood a few feet behind him.

Jacob examined his dad's body—the IV stand, heart monitor, and other medical devices shackled him in a way. Jacob rubbed the back of his neck as he walked around to the other side of the bed. Bill approached the bed.

Jacob placed his scarf and coat over the back of the rocking chair, removed the items from the chair down to the floor, then sat down beside his dad's bed. He rocked a few times all the time staring at his dad. Bill noticed Jacob's face had gone pale. Jacob leaned in and took his dad's hand.

"Your hand is cold," Jacob mumbled.

Bill's heart melted as he looked the old bed-ridden man over. He had bed sores on his elbow, a slack jaw with a tube hanging from his mouth, and a nasal oxygen tube which pulsed bursts of air out of rhythm with the raspy breath he took each time he inhaled. Bill felt uncomfortable, intrusive. He stepped around the nightstand beside the bed. Just as he reached it, a digital thermometer fell to the floor.

Crash! Jacob's head snapped up.

"I'm sorry," Bill whispered, feeling ashamed.

"This isn't easy for me." Jacob looked right through Bill.

"I'm really, really sorry," Bill apologized again. "Please go ahead."

"Dad, the nurse just told me some bad news." Jacob shook his head and looked directly into his dad's pale face.

Bill noticed Jacob's face contorting in a mixture of angry sorrow—tender eyes contrasted by a clinched jaw and pursed lips.

Jacob dropped his face onto the mattress, silent for a moment. Then he suddenly stood and turned his back to the bed. Bill watched his every move.

"I need," Jacob turned around. "I need to talk to you, Dad. But I don't really even know if you can hear me."

"Jacob," Bill whispered. "your dad is ill, but I'm certain that somehow he can hear you. Go ahead. Tell him what's in your heart. Pretend that he's just resting with his eyes closed."

"I'm just going to talk. You listen, Dad." Jacob slowly returned to the chair and took his dad's hand again, holding it sandwiched between his own hands. "I don't really know where to start.

"I never took the time to tell you how much I looked up to you," Jacob muttered. "My whole life I wanted to be as loving and nurturing as you." Jacob pulled his dad's hand close to his lips. "My entire life, I wanted to grow up and become half the great man you were." A tear fell from Jacob's face onto his dad's fingers. Bill's eyes filled with his own grief-born tears.

"I had such dreams of spending years and years with you and Mom. You retired and built the cabin. We started our family. Then Mom died so unexpectedly." Jacob inhaled deep then let it out.

"Today, Shelly saw a picture of Mom and wanted to sit on her lap, but . . ." Jacob cried. "I can't do this." Jacob returned his dad's hand to the bed and rose to his feet.

"Jacob, you can do this," Bill reassured in a calm and supportive voice. "Just don't rush things. Just say whatever you can say right now."

"Dad," Jacob put both hands in his pockets. "I could always come to you for advice. I need some now."

"Ask him. Go ahead." Bill urged.

"Lately, things aren't going well in the family, the marriage, the office." Jacob studied his dad's face again. "I know you. You could tell me what to do if you could speak." Jacob's face surrendered a faint and brief smile. "It just feels like everything I knew and loved is gone. I feel so lost without you and Mom. I mean *you're* here, but not really."

"I hate Alzheimer's. It keeps you in front of us. But it silently steals your life from within. Before you got sick, people looked up to you so much. When you first checked into the hospital, there were hundreds of cards and always fresh flowers." Jacob looked at the bare walls. "But you changed. People quit coming to see you because you became so mean spirited." He shook his head.

"Anyway, you may not remember this, but you did some very funny things at first. Ha! You forgot your own name at the supermarket checkout line. You held up the checker for ten minutes, insisting that you could sign your own name to the check. You just couldn't remember it and you refused to believe in the name she repeatedly called you. That was when you and I both knew something bad was happening." Jacob drew closer to the bed.

"Dad, the worst of all the weird things you did was the Macareña dance." Jacob nodded his head. "Yes, I think the town is still in recovery from that little episode. You stood in the middle of the fountain, just outside this hospital here, and you did the best Macareña rendition a sixty-year-old man ever performed in a public fountain. I left you in jail that night because I had no idea what to do for you." Bill walked over to stand behind Jacob.

"I know this isn't very pleasant, but I also need to tell you about how you hurt us: Nancy, Shelly, and me." Jacob's hands trembled as he pulled them out of his pockets. "When you moved into our home, we had to make some big adjustments."

"You see, you did things, hurtful things. Once you lit the Christmas tree on fire because you thought there was a crow in its branches. It scared Shelly to be around Christmas trees, so we haven't had a tree since then. You often left the front door wide open when you walked away during the middle of the night." Jacob turned away toward the window. Bill walked with him.

"Then the abuse started." Jacob tensed both of his fists, rubbing his thumbs across his knuckles. "You called Nancy a Jezebel all the time. You kept telling me she was having an affair with a man in a trenchcoat. You called her a prostitute more than once, Dad. Nancy was my wife and best friend. I couldn't stand it." Jacob marched over to the window.

Bill couldn't believe what he heard about this gentle, frail old man.

"Then you started spanking Shelly. You said she stole your wallet!" Jacob raised his voice and slammed both clenched fists down to the window sill. "I would have bought ten new wallets for you if only it would have helped." Jacob breathed hard as he stood tensed from head to toe. Bill stood close by.

"We took you into our home, because we couldn't make ourselves put you in a nursing home. We still can't. We pay a fortune to keep you in this hospital." Jacob turned to face toward his dad, fists still clenched.

"That's when you started to steal the life of my marriage and family." Jacob lunged forward grabbing the metal frame of the bed, causing it to screech a few inches across the floor. "I hope to God we can recover from it," he wailed as he released the frame of his dad's bed and fell to his knees.

"I never could have known, Jacob," Bill whispered. "Never. And I'm certain that your dad didn't know either. I've got this gut feeling that he couldn't have known. Think about it, Jacob." Bill moved to Jacob's side. "Think about how your dad was before the disease struck. He was loving and caring for all those years. Then suddenly this. It's Alzheimer's, not your dad," Bill assured. Jacob slowly pulled himself back up to his feet.

"Jacob," a thought suddenly occurred to Bill. "the only way for you to recover is to forgive. You must try to forgive your dad. For your own sake, let it go." Jacob's anger fell from his face at that moment. Jacob walked back to his dad's side, holding his hand again.

"Did you, Dad? Did you even know what you did to us? All that incessant walking and fidgeting, all the strange behaviors, all the twenty-four hours per day monitoring as things got worse and worse and worse," Jacob whispered. "I said it was abuse, but how could it have been abuse?" Jacob collapsed forward and buried his face in the pillow next to his dad's face.

"Lord, help me." He prayed. "Help me to forgive my dad, please." He prayed aloud.

"Just say it, Jacob. Just say, I forgive you, Dad. The rest will follow," Bill whispered.

"I want to forgive you, Dad. And I pray that you can hear me." Jacob raised his face up out of the pillow next to his dad's ear. "I . . . forgive . . . you." An expression of peace settled into

Jacob's face.

"I know he heard you, Jacob. I can't explain how, but I'm sure of it." Jacob climbed up onto the bed, beside his dad. He held his dad's hand next to his heart and silently cried.

Bill felt reverent as though he'd witnessed something sacred. As he moved to the foot of the bed, he suddenly became fully aware of the pain that had haunted him in the darkness. It sat in his chest like a gallon-sized bucket, filled to the top with toxic black emptiness and loss. He knew the contents of this bucket all too well. It poisoned his soul each time he lay trapped on his own hospital bed in the darkness.

Bill thought he knew how to handle his pain. He walked over to the window to see if any children played outside. Only a few had sleds, but they headed home. He felt the contents of the bucket begin to boil. It always boiled just before the darkness came.

Oh, no, I'm not with Pat. The darkness knows I'm alone. He spun around, frantic about avoiding the darkness. *Help me, Lord. Help me, please. I don't want to go back to the darkness.* He covered his face. *I want to stay here with Jacob.*

Bill had another sudden impression. He reached out and gently put his hands on Jacob's and his dad's feet. At that moment the bucket began to empty in a small stream that flowed out of his chest, down his sleeves, and into a puddle on the floor. Bill felt his life force strengthen at the same time the darkness weakened. Soon, the near empty bucket stopped draining into the puddle. Bill let go of their feet and stepped back, watching the puddle evaporate until it had entirely disappeared.

"I miss you so much. I love you so much. Please know this." Jacob kissed his dad's forehead and hugged him. Jacob then stood, walked back to the window, and stared out at the grounds. Bill noticed Jacob's peaceful expression, a striking contrast to when he'd first came into his dad's room. Jacob walked back to his dad's side and gave him one last kiss on the hand.

"You'll be happy to know we're spending Christmas up at

the cabin. I'm sure it's what you and Mom would have us do."

"Your dad loves you, too, Jacob. I just know it within myself," said Bill.

Jacob reached down and picked up the things from the floor and put them back in the chair. He draped his coat and scarf over his arm then walked to the door. Bill walked beside him. Jacob sighed, looking back at his dad. He turned out the light and walked down the long hallway. Bill followed. As they reached the ER, Pat stood waiting by the cafeteria. Jacob stopped to put on his coat and scarf.

"How did it go in there?" Pat whispered as she and Bill stepped into the cafeteria.

"Rough at first. I had no idea what all had happened, but I think Jacob forgave enough to begin to heal."

"Oh, I'm so happy to hear that." Pat looked back at Jacob. "I'm so happy. Nancy and Shelly need him back in their lives."

"Shouldn't we go with Jacob? He just walked out the door."

"Not yet, Bill. I made arrangements for you. We need to meet with your memory recovery specialist." Pat and Bill went downstairs to the Cowboy Room.

Nine

What's Up, Bill?

"HOW ARE you, Bill?" asked Nadia as he walked into the Cowboy Room and sat at the same round table. A stethoscope and blood pressure cuff sat atop a white lab coat on top of the table. They faced one another across it.

"I feel a little better."

"Better about what?"

"About Jacob."

"He just helped Jacob work things out with his dad," Pat explained.

"I see." Nadia made a note on her clipboard.

"I think Jacob forgave his dad."

"He did?" Nadia inquired, glancing quickly over to Pat. "And?"

"And I remember it all."

"All of what?"

"All of Jacob's feelings he shared with his dad."

"Oh." Nadia's voice had the sound of disappointment in it.

"Oh?" Bill asked loudly. "I remembered what just happened in pretty good detail. I remembered you, Nadia. I'm better."

"Better doesn't mean whole," Nadia explained. "You still have more recovery to make. I'm sorry to give you the news."

"Is she telling the truth, Pat?"

"Yes," Pat reassured. "You've exceeded our expectations with how quickly you have recovered so far."

"I have?"

"Absolutely." Nadia flipped through the pages on her clipboard. "I've reported your progress to the highest authority. They are very pleased."

"They are?"

"Yes, but now I need to ask you some more questions. Is that okay with you, Bill?"

"I guess. Go ahead, Nadia."

"Do you remember what you did for a living, I mean before you came to the hospital?"

"Well, let me think." He closed his eyes. His mind wandered to glowing ornaments, colored lights, and a green tree in the middle of the huge hangar. He shook his head.

"Perhaps, you could look for a package wrapped in shiny paper under the tree," Nadia instructed. "Do you see it?"

Bill nodded.

"Describe it to us."

"It's about the size of shoe box, wrapped in gold paper with golden ribbon and a bow."

"Unwrap it, Bill," Pat urged.

"It's a stethoscope and . . . and a head piece with grey bunny rabbit ears. Oh!"

"What is it, Bill?" Asked Nadia.

"It's hundreds of small children sitting on hundreds of examination tables."

"Well, say hello to them."

"Hi, kids." Bill smiled.

"What's up, Doc?" The children replied in chorus." Bill jumped back in his seat. "I'm a . . . I was a pediatrician. I specialized in treating children."

"That's right," Pat explained. "You taught the children to always greet you with the phrase, What's up, Doc. You even had long bunny ears you wore around the office."

"I did. I remember now, I cared for children for three decades." Bill sat back and smiled in his rich memories of his medical practice. Pat and Nadia sat quietly and allowed him the experience. Eventually, Bill opened his eyes again.

"What's up, Doc?" Pat held her pointed fingers above her ears like bunny ears.

"You are, ya silly wabbit." Bill made the same gesture with his hands. Pat smiled. Nadia made a quick note on the clipboard. "Pat, is this my stethoscope?" Bill looked closely at the one on the table.

"No, but you had one just like it."

"I have to leave for now. That means we'll need another visit."

"Can't you please finish before you go? I so want you to finish before Christmas morning," Pat supplicated.

"I'm sorry, Pat. He needs a bit more experience with the Wilsons first. We can't rush these things too much." Pat lowered her head. "But perhaps . . ."

"Perhaps?"

"Perhaps we can meet soon."

"The Wilsons," Bill mused aloud. "Now why are they connected to the pediatric practice I had all those years? Did I treat Shelly?"

"Yes, you did." Nadia placed her pen on the clipboard.

"Bill, I have to trust Nadia's expertise. If you need to work with the Wilsons, then let's get to it." Pat rose to her feet. "We're going up to the cabin, Nadia," Pat explained.

"Wonderful."

Bill could tell that Pat felt upset. He noticed that Nadia observed her behavior now instead of his.

"Listen, Pat." Nadia tapped on the clipboard. "I'll rearrange my schedule to meet you later at the cabin." Nadia rose and walked out the door.

"When?" Pat called out as Nadia turned the corner and ascended the stairs.

"Tonight, Christmas Eve," Nadia yelled back.

"Thank you, Nadia." Pat whispered, looking relieved.

"Pat, was I a good pediatrician?"

"I think so, Bill." Pat adjusted her already neat clothes. "You saved all the children that could be saved. Many others got better because of your expertise."

"But . . ."

"What, Bill?"

"Did the children like me?"

"Almost." Pat walked toward the door.

"Almost?" His eyes opened wide as he followed.

"Almost as much as you liked them. Come on, ya silly wabbit."

☙ ❧

They traveled quickly to the Wilsons' home. The green SUV sat curbside on the street, with grocery sacks and suitcases loaded in the back. Nancy and Shelly stood next to it while Jacob locked the front door of the house. Pat and Bill stood beside Shelly, who held her two dolls like newborn babies in her arms.

"I'm so glad you could join us in the Christmas cabin," Shelly whispered to her dolls.

"We're glad, too," Pat replied. Bill nodded.

"Are we ready, then?" Jacob opened the door for Shelly. "Let's have our distinguished guests ride in the back seat with you." Shelly climbed in and slid all the way over to the other side, holding her dolls in her hands. Bill and Pat sat next to her. Jacob took Nancy by the hand around to the other side of the SUV. He opened the front door for her. Nancy climbed in. Jacob closed Nancy's door and watched her through the window.

"Daddy, I'm buckled in." Shelly called out.

Jacob just kept looking at Nancy.

"Daddy, I'll catch a cold if we don't shut the door." Shelly impatiently called.

Nancy finally caught on and looked out at Jacob. He smiled then came around to shut Shelly's door then sit in the driver's seat. He inserted the key, but didn't crank it.

"What is it, Jacob?"

"Are you two ready for a special surprise?"

"Surprise?" Shelly hugged her dolls.

"What did you do, Jacob?" Nancy placed her hand gently onto his arm. Jacob reached into his coat packet and pulled out a remote control.

"Ladies, I give you the Wilson Christmas lights." He pressed the button and the outside Christmas lights came on. Their red and green, yellow and white, blue and orange lights framed the entire roof line, balcony, porch, garage, and windows in a breathtaking array.

"Wahoo!" Shelly climbed across Pat and Bill, rubbing the fog from the window with her sleeve. "We got a Christmas house now. Huh, Daddy?"

"Yes, we do."

"Just like a family," Shelly added.

"They're beautiful, Jacob. How and when did you get the lights to work?" Nancy asked.

"Does it matter?"

"I guess not. Thank you for the lights, Jacob." Nancy squeezed his arm for a brief moment.

"Buckle up, Shelly. We're going to the Christmas cabin."

"Okay, Daddy." Shelly climbed back into her seat. Jacob cranked the SUV and drove down the street. Pat looked at Bill with a sweet smile on her face.

☙ Ten ❧

Christmas Cabin

THE DRIVE up to the cabin took hours, because the snow fell heavy during the first half of the trip. Jacob filled the time with details of his visit with his dad. He remembered almost all of the detail. Bill remembered them all and felt a bit of relief from Jacob's healing. By nightfall, they'd reached the top of the mountain. The snows had stopped falling. The clouds had cleared.

"We're here." Jacob announced as he pulled near to the shore of the first of Payson's many small lakes.

"Where's the cabin, Daddy?" Shelly unbuckled and stood to look out her window.

"The cabin's a bit further up the road, Shelly." Jacob sighed. "You know, it feels like a lifetime since I've seen this lake in the winter."

Bill looked out his window. The lake looked a bit larger than a football field. Naked quaking aspen trees hedged it shoreline. Behind the aspens, thick clusters of lodge-pole pines stood tall, thick, and green against the snow. Bill felt peace.

"Buckle up, Shelly. We'll be at the cabin in a few minutes." Nancy reached back over the seat to help her. "I can't wait for you to see it."

"I can't wait to see it again." Jacob added as he drove on up the road.

Bill soaked in the wintery, mountain scene outside his car window. They passed another lake, then another.

"As beautiful as it always has been," Nancy whispered, holding Jacob's hand.

"I'd almost forgotten."

"Forgotten what, Daddy?"

"How peaceful I feel up here." Jacob replied as he drove further down a side road that led to the cabin community. He turned left up the hill about a hundred feet off the main road, then parked in the driveway of the cabin. The headlights illuminated the front of the cabin. Everybody stared at it through the windshield. Snow piled on both sides of its two-story, steep A-frame roof. A large window looked onto the small porch that faced the big east lake down the hill. The second floor had two smaller windows. Bill wanted to go inside to see the interior.

"Jacob." Nancy exclaimed, opening her car door. "It's absolutely beautiful!"

The others joined her, looking out across the view of the beautiful valley below. The bright moon illuminated the grey hued snow which covered the landscape.

"Look, Nancy." Jacob pointed down to the lake. "A doe and her fawn."

"They are precious, Jacob." Nancy whispered, picking Shelly up into her arms. "Do you see them, Shelly?"

Shelly nodded.

"Shelly, I remember the very first year your daddy and I came up here. We saw a small heard crossing the frozen lake. Do you remember that, Jacob?"

"Yeah. And I remember you. You were so excited to be up here, to be with my parents, to be an extended family."

"It feels the exact same way to me, now, Jacob." Nancy went up to him and put her arm around his waist.

"Look at all those up there," Shelly pointed to the sky.

"Stars, look at the millions of stars," said Jacob.

"Well, why don't we have them like that at our house, Daddy?"

"The city lights are so bright that you can't see them all, but Payson has lots of stars, too."

"Really?"

"Yes," Nancy added. "The stars are always there. They watch down on us even if sometimes we simply can't see them."

They star-gazed a few minutes longer, gathered Shelly's dolls and backpack, then walked up to the porch.

"Daddy, I think your mouth needs a muffler. You're making smoke." Shelly giggled. Jacob blew a long breath of fog toward her. This made her giggle even more. Bill and Pat stood below the porch, watching the three of them. Bill noticed the sad expressions that snuck in between Jacob's laughter and words.

"Are you okay, Jacob?"

"Nancy," Jacob turned around in a complete circle. "Nancy, I'm as okay as I can be. It's been years." Jacob forced a smile.

"I know," Nancy answered. "There are lots of memories for us up here. Most of them buried by the last few painful years."

"Hello, I'm gonna turn into a popsicle if we don't go inside," said Shelly.

"You think so, huh?" Nancy tweaked Shelly's nose. "What do you say, Jacob. Shall we make some new memories?"

"Yeah, let's make some new ones." Jacob opened the door. "Ladies, welcome to the Wilson's Christmas cabin." Jacob stepped inside. The motion detector on the light switch turned the lights on inside the livingroom and kitchen. Nancy carried Shelly inside as Bill and Pat followed.

"Oh, my." Nancy exclaimed.

"Oh, boy!" Shelly ran in and placed her backpack and dolls on the sofa. "Look, look! It's the three wise guys." Shelly pointed to statues on the hearth.

"I think you mean the three wise men, Shelly." Nancy took them down and placed them on the coffee table so Shelly could see them up close. "Jacob, did Charlie come up earlier today?"

"Yeah, I called him this morning."

"He built a fire. The coals are still glowing."

"He set the table, too." They looked at the plates, utensils, glasses, candlestick, bottle of sparkling cider, and homemade bread. "What is that delicious smell?" Jacob walked over to the oven and opened it. He put on oven mitts then pulled the large pan out, placing it onto the stove. When he lifted the lid steam rushed out, filling the air with a wonderful smell.

"It's turkey," Shelly announced.

"And the pop-up timer is out. It's ready to eat." Jacob sat it on the table.

"Jacob, look." Nancy walked over to the counter. "Two fresh pumpkin pies. I'm sure Charlie's wife made them. I love pumpkin pie." Nancy clasped both hands together in front of her smiling face. They sat down and immediately started to eat.

Christmas Eve dinner sounded quiet to Bill—lots of eating, not much talking. But he knew the difference in this quiet and the quite they'd had before. Bill felt especially happy that Nancy ate a regular portion of everything and two pieces of pie.

After dinner, Nancy and Shelly sat on the plush rug in front of the coffee table. Jacob made a few trips to unload the SUV. Bill followed him each time. He felt drawn to protect Jacob, maybe because of having watched him in the hospital room with his dad, maybe because he sensed Jacob's vulnerability. Either way, he shadowed him attentively. Once everything had been unloaded, Bill sat on the couch next to Pat. Jacob joined the others on the rug. Shelly sat between her parents, holding her two dolls.

"Mommy, could Jim and Chrissy play with the three wise guys . . . I mean wise men?"

"Oh, no, Shelly. Those are too fragile to play with. Besides, your granddad used them to tell a wonderful story to us every Christmas Eve."

"Tell me the story, please," Shelly begged.

Nancy looked at Jacob. He shrugged and moved to the opposite side of the coffee table arranging things. Shelly and Nancy sat up next to the table on the other side. Pat scooted a bit closer to Bill.

"Now, be patient with me, ladies. This is my first time ever telling this one." Jacob cleared his throat. "A long time ago, when the very first Christmas was actually taking place, there were three wise men . . ."

"Daddy, you have only two wise men in your hands."

"He's getting to that, Shelly." Nancy hugged her.

"Anyway, the time of Jesus' birth had come and the bright new Christmas star appeared in the night sky."

"They had stars just like us, huh?"

"Yes, they did, but this star was really, really bright and it let the wise men know what had happened. The two wise men gathered their belongings for the long trip to see the baby Jesus, but the third wise man could not be found."

"Was he lost?"

"Yes; the other two looked in the markets, in the orchards, and by the sea shore. They just couldn't find him. If they didn't leave soon, then it might be too late." Jacob spoke in a concerned tone.

"Oh, no. What did they do? Did they leave the third wise man and go without him?"

"No, Shelly. You see, the wise men were life-long friends. They knew that something very special had happened in the world when the Christmas star appeared."

"So, what did they do?"

"Well, in the middle of the last possible night before they'd have to leave, they decided to go to the third wise man's palace. When they got to the gates, they saw a man in a white cape, running across the courtyard and into the servant's quarters."

"The third wise man lived in a palace?"

"Yes, all of the wise men were kings and had palaces and many servants. Anyway, the man in the robe finally ran from the servants' quarters and saw the two wise men at the gate. He ran up to talk to them."

"Was he a robber?"

"No, no, turns out he was the third wise man." Jacob placed the third statue on the coffee table.

"Really?"

"Yes, and he explained that when he saw the Christmas star, he felt so much joy at Jesus' birth that he secretively delivered a gift to everyone in the palace—every servant, every guard, and every family member. He became the first wise man."

"That sounds fun." Shelly smiled.

"Oh, it was fun. In fact, the wise men decided then and there that they would gather their most precious belongings and bring them to give to the baby Jesus as a gift."

"Were those the first Christmas gifts?"

"No, Shelly. They were the second Christmas gifts."

Bill watched Shelly furrow her tiny brow, sorting it all out.

"I get it." She smiled. "The baby Jesus was the first Christmas gift, huh?"

"Yes." Jacob smiled. "The first and most important gift the earth has ever received." Jacob leaned across the table, kissed Shelly on the forehead, and kissed Nancy on the lips. Bill and Pat smiled, still sitting on the couch.

"Jacob, you told that story just like Dad used to tell it."

"Thanks, Nancy."

"Merry Christmas, friend."

"Merry Christmas, friend." Jacob kissed Nancy's hand.

"Merry Christmas." Shelly stood and hugged her mommy then walked around and hugged her daddy.

"Jacob, the fire's burning out." Nancy laid her head down on her folded arms which rested on the coffee table. Shelly knelt beside her with her arm around her neck.

"I'll get some more firewood." Jacob stood up and walked through the kitchen out the back door of the cabin. Shelly caressed her mommy's hair.

"That was a fine Christmas story, Pat," Bill whispered as he folded his arms and tried to remember past Christmas Eves.

"I liked it too, Bill."

"Nancy!" Jacob called, struggling to get the door open. "Nancy!" She jumped up and ran to the door. When she opened it for him, he came through with a large box full of wrapped gifts.

"What in the world?" Nancy covered her mouth. "Did you do this?"

"No, these were in the storage room, on top of the firewood. Look, there's a note from Charlie." Jacob sat the presents down.

"We get presents?" Shelly ran over to join them. "Wahoo!" She clapped her hands.

"This will be good, Bill. Watch," Pat whispered as they both watched from the sofa.

Jacob read the note aloud.

Dear Wilsons:
I've had these presents for years.
I promised your mom before she died that I would put them
under the tree on the next Christmas Eve at the cabin.
Well, it's been a long time hasn't it? Your mom left a present
for each of you and for your dad. Bless his heart.
Merry Christmas,
Charlie

"Oh, Jacob. We have presents for Christmas after all. And they're from Mom!" Nancy hugged him. Jacob looked pained, yet happy. Bill wanted to go stand next to him. He started to get up.

"Stay here next to me, Bill." Pat looked up to him tenderly. Bill stayed.

"These presents have been up here this entire time and I didn't know it," Jacob regretfully whispered.

"Daddy, you got the biggest present. Open it, please," Shelly begged.

"Do, Jacob. Open yours first." Nancy helped him pull it from the box. It must have been a foot wide and four feet long. Jacob took the note and read it aloud.

Dearest Jacob,
Youre opening this present now because
I am no longer there with you. I talked Dad into
letting me give this to you under these circumstances.

When your dad was just a boy, he and his
father built this from scratch. Its priceless.
I'm always with you.
Love, Your secret wise man, Mom

Jacob gently removed the faded wrapping paper from the large gift. In it he found a hand-carved solid oak sled with metal runners. Bill's eyes lit up as he looked at Pat. She raised her shoulders, smiling and sharing in his excitement.

"Wow, a sled!" Shelly clapped her hands again.

"'William III.' It reads 'William III,'" Jacob explained.

"I don't understand." Nancy ran her hand across the wood surface of the sled.

"You see, Great-grandfather was named William. And Grandfather was also named William, the second and Dad was . . ."

"William III." Nancy smiled.

"Can you take me sledding on this, Daddy?"

"Sure, tomorrow, Shelly."

"But, didn't Mom say this was priceless?" Nancy asked.

"Yes, she did. But, it's priceless because Shelly will ride it with us. Mom and Dad didn't believe in making museum pieces out of sleds," Jacob placed the sled beside the front door.

"Open your present, Mommy." Shelly handed the square, flat gift to Nancy. Nancy opened it to find a beautiful pot holder and a note.

Nancy, for years you treated me like your own mother.
I feel that you are like the daughter I never had.
As you use this, think of me and remember our
happy times together. Its the most loving gift
I could give to you. Its priceless. But please try
to remember that we dont believe in making
museum pieces out of potholders. Its our way.
Love, Your secret wise man, Mom

Nancy finished reading the note. She held the potholder over her heart while she hugged Jacob and Shelly. She then reached into the box and handed a small rectangular shaped gift to Shelly.

"Now you open yours, Shelly." Nancy stood beside Jacob as Shelly tore into her present. Shelly looked at it, eyes and mouth wide opened.

"Oh, look." She held up a three inch marble carved figurine of the baby Jesus, lying in a manger. "It's beautiful." Shelly hugged it. "I love it. Thank you, Grandmom, thank you."

"Did Shelly get a note?" Nancy asked.

"Let me see . . . here it is, it fell off into the box." Jacob opened it and read it aloud.

Shelly, you are such a precious little girl.
I look into your baby blue eyes and think I see
a piece of heaven in your soul. I want to be there
with you in all the important times of your life.
But heaven cant wait for me to come home,
so I promise you Ill be there when you read this note
and Ill be there for you every time you need me.
Love, your secret wise man, Grandmom

"Do you see her?" Shelly looked around the kitchen. "I don't."

"She's here." Jacob confirmed looking around.

"Yes, she is," Nancy added.

"How do you know? I don't see her." Shelly looked again.

"Shelly." Nancy lifted Shelly up to hold her. "Whenever your grandmom made a promise, she always kept it. That's the way she was."

"It's true, Shelly," Jacob added.

"I wish I could sit in her lap and thank her for our presents."

"Me, too, Shelly. Me, too." Jacob consoled. Bill smiled. Pat sat quietly.

"Hey, there's an envelope with a card. Who is it for?" Nancy tried to hand it to Jacob. "Perfume." He refused it, covering his nose.

"Oh, look. There's a posty note on the letter." Nancy read it.

Whomever reads this note first.
Please open the envelope and let this note air for a while.
I spilled enough of my perfume on it
to set off Dads and Jacobs allergies.

"She did, ladies. Even after all these years." Jacob coughed and hacked.

Nancy opened it up, placing it on the kitchen counter by the back door.

Jacob and Nancy took Shelly upstairs to bed. Bill and Pat remained on the couch. Soon, the cabin fell silent. Bill and Pat saw the last glow of the ambers disappear in the pile of grey fireplace ashes.

"This was the best Christmas Eve I can remember." Bill felt relaxed, stretched out on the couch.

"And just how many can you remember?" Pat chided.

"One. Hey, that's a great improvement from just a few days ago."

"I agree. You know, I remember all my Christmas Eves. This one's my favorite."

"It has been exciting so far, hasn't it?" Nadia added. Bill and Pat spun around to find Nadia standing behind the sofa.

"Oh, Nadia. I'm sorry, we didn't hear you come in." Pat apologized.

"It's good to be with you. Look, I'm sorry to say that I must hurry because of another critical engagement. So, let's get to work. Can we talk at the kitchen table?" Bill sat at the end of the table, Pat sat to his right and Nadia sat to his left. Shelly had brought the photo of the entire family and left it on the table. It sat face up, showing Jacob, Nancy, Grandmom holding Shelly on her lap, and Granddad.

"Bill, do you recognize any of the people in that photo?"

"Let's see, uh, there's Shelly, Nancy, and Jacob. And there's Shelly's grandmom and granddad."

"Good. Do you know their names?"

"Who, the grandparents?"

"Yes, who is that beautiful woman and that strikingly handsome man?" Nadia pointed to each in the photo. Bill studied them, looking to Pat for a clue. She shrugged her shoulders.

"Maybe, we can try another avenue on this one. Bill, what is the relationship between Jacob and the older man in this photo?"

"Let's see, Jacob is his son. That's his dad."

"Excellent. Can we start there this time?"

"Fine with me."

"Now, close your eyes and go back in your mind to the hangar."

Bill closed his eyes and started waving.

"Bill, who are you waving to?" Asked Nadia.

"Oh, just all the children, sitting on the examination tables. They appear to be waiting for something."

"Fine, that's just fine. Now, Bill walk all the way through the hangar, where the children and tables end."

Bill nodded.

"Do you see any wooden items?"

"Yes, here's Balsa-wood snowflake. It looks hand-painted white. It has a handwritten note glued to the front of it."

"Good, read the note," Nadia requested.

"Out loud, please, I'd like to hear it," Pat asked.

"It reads: To Dad, my loving father. From Jacob. Christmas Eve, 1986."

> FATHER is a special word to me at Christmas time.
> F is for the best friend a son could ever have.
> A is for the angels, who watched over us when we sled.
> T is for together—Dad, Mom, and me.
> H is for happy, how I feel on Christmas Eve.
> E is for early, when I woke you on Christmas day.
> R is for remember that my love for your will always stay.

"Bill, now, place the snowflake onto the limbs of the tree," Nadia instructed.

"I did. It belongs there, doesn't it?" Bill opened his eyes.

"Yes, Bill it does," Pat replied, smiling.

"Nadia, is this snowflake mine?"

"Yes."

"Is this, Jacob, I mean the one, here in this cabin, is he my son?"

"What do you think, Bill?"

"I think he is."

"You're right. Close your eyes."

Bill closed his eyes again and saw another quarter of his hangar light up in an explosion of brilliant light. "Oh, mercy," Bill exclaimed.

"Bill, can you describe what you see as you walk through this portion of the hangar?"

"Well, I see adoption papers framed on my wall. Jacob was adopted."

"That's right. He's adopted," Pat confirmed.

"I see his kindergarten graduation diploma, his Eagle Scout award, his junior pilot's club patch, and his high school diploma."

"You kept all of these framed on your office wall at the clinic."

"I did, Pat. I did. Wait—here's his marriage certificate to Nancy and his CPA license. Oh, look, here's Shelly's birth certificate and baby pictures." His heart sank in his chest. Tears flowed down his cheeks. He said nothing for a while.

"Bill, what do you see?" Pat whispered.

"Jacob, in the hospital room, talking to his dad." Bill shook his head. "I'm so ashamed of how I hurt him."

"Open your eyes." Nadia instructed.

"Okay."

"Do you remember the most important thing Jacob did in that hospital room."

"Yes. He forgave his dad." Bill wiped his eyes with his sleeve.

"He forgave *you,* Bill. You just didn't know it yet."

"He did, Nadia. He forgave me."

"Now you must forgive." Pat leaned across the table.

"Forgive who?"

"Yourself, Bill." Pat nodded.

Bill cried for a while, closing his eyes more out of embarrassment than therapy.

"Do you see anything more?" Pat asked after he stopped crying.

"Nothing, Pat. I'm at the end of Jacob's portion of my hangar and half of it still sits in pitch blackness." Bill opened his eyes. Pat's strained, trying to smile. "I'm sorry Pat. I know you must feel frustrated by my slowness."

"But, we're making great progress. We're almost done."

"Pat's right. Now, one last thing, you already know the location of the last decoration for the tree."

"I do?"

"Yes, you do." Close your eyes again. "Pat, would you recite for Bill the note you wrote for Shelly's Christmas present?"

"Certainly. 'Shelly, you are such a precious little girl . . .'" Pat recited.

"Pat wrote the note?" Bill questioned aloud. "Pat, I'm Jacob's dad, you're Jacob's mom, and that means we're . . ." He peaked out of one eye. Pat smiled sweetly back to him.

"Please close both eyes, Bill."

"Look, on the top of my Christmas tree, a beautiful angel dressed in white from head to toe. The rest of the hangar is brightly lit now. Pat, you and I are . . ."

"Married, Bill. I'm your wife, Squeaky the clown."

"You told me you had another man."

"I did have another man. It's the real Bill Wilson. It's you," Pat explained. He opened his eyes to meet hers. They smiled.

"Bill, I know this may sound rude, but keep your eyes closed. You need to walk through this part of the hangar in order to completely recover your memory." He reluctantly closed them again.

"Tell me, friend, what do you see in my part of the hangar?" Pat whispered.

"It's not just what I see, Pat. I feel your loving presence in every inch of this hangar."

"Look, I see, you and me in medical school. You're sitting at the reception desk of the admissions office. I overheard you when you told the other secretary that I was cute. . . . Wait, there's our marriage license, medical school graduation, first home deed, first new car title, adoption application, picture of you and me holding Jacob at the airport, our thirty-year anniversary cruise to Alaska." He continued, recounting event after life event. Pat confirmed his memories as he recited them aloud

"Oh, no, no." Bill felt the pain in his chest.

"What is it?"

"It's a coffin. I think it's your coffin." He strained to inhale as he choked up. "I lost part of my soul the day you died."

"I know, Bill. You always had the biggest most tender heart in the world," Pat consoled. Bill rested his elbows on the kitchen table and covered his teary eyes with his hands.

"Goodbye, Doc," the children called to Bill in unison.

"Bye, kids," Bill replied as he opened his eyes. Most of the remaining darkness drained and evaporated as it had before.

"Pat, I need a big hug."

"Not yet, Bill," Nadia interjected.

"Nadia's right. We can hug later."

"Merry Christmas, Pat and Bill." Nadia whispered as the sun broke over the top of the mountain range outside the window.

"Merry Christmas," they replied.

"I have to go. Bill, you no longer need my help." Nadia stood. It truly has been an honor, working with you. Soon, your entire life will unfold to you in the totality of all the smallest details."

"Will we need to meet again for that?"

"No, Bill. You and Pat will be alone for that moment."

"Nadia, Pat, I feel I need to apologize."

"Whatever for, Bill?" Pat inquired.

"I flirted with both of you over the last couple of days. It was rude and disrespectful."

"Don't give it another thought. Lot's of people suffering as you did will flirt in their recovery phase."

"I was a doctor. I should have behaved better."

"Oh, doctors know very little about this part of Alzheimer's recovery. You can't blame them. They only see the mortal side of it all." Nadia walked over to the door. "You two may stay a bit longer, but I must go."

Bill and Pat sat back down on the couch. A warm ray of sunlight came through the window and bathed the living room. Jacob and Nancy descended the stairs. Bill could hear Shelly playing in her room upstairs. Nancy heated a pan on the stove while Jacob poured water in the pancake mix. As he stirred the batter, he picked up the note, still airing out on the counter. He smelled it.

"Has it aired out enough for you to read, Jacob?"

"I think so." He sniffed it. "Take over the batter for a minute." Jacob wiped his hand on his robe.

"I've been waiting for this part. Listen carefully to the note, Bill." Pat came over to the edge of the kitchen.

"Okay, Pat." Bill followed.

Dearest Bill,
The night you collapsed in the hospital I cried myself to sleep.
In my dreams, your father came to warn me of the
difficult times the Wilsons would soon face. He also
showed me how I can help everyone get through it.
So heres my Christmas gift to you: I promise you that
I will come back for you. Just like the two wise men,
searching for their best friend, Ill come find you.
Until then, all my love,
Your secret wise man, Pat

"Jacob, that is so very sweet." Nancy looked over Jacob's shoulder.

"I bet she did come back for him. I bet she did." Jacob showed her the note.

☙ ❧

"Pat?" Bill turned to find her gone. "Pat?" he called out as the cabin disappeared.

Eleven

Christmas Morning

"NOT AGAIN, not again." Bill laid motionless in an isolated hospital bed. He sat in what felt like a soundless, lightless, and peopleless empty room. "Help." He called out. "Help me, somebody." His voice echoed back to him. He lingered ever so lonely and painfully here. His pain felt unbearable. It came from deep inside his chest and tortured him with an emptiness and nagging feeling of loss. He'd call out, but no one answered. No one ever attended his needs. The only constant he now could count on, turned out to be what he came to refer to as the darkness.

Bill felt the pain from the gallon-sized bucket again. He felt its presence in his chest, but it felt light, less threatening. He looked into its emptiness. It had all drained out, all but one small blob that sat recessed in the bottom of the bucket.

Bill had another sudden impression in his heart. He decided to follow it, so he closed his eyes and prayed, "*Oh Lord, please free me from this darkness, please.*"

"What's up, Doc?" A child's voice called out to him.

"You, ya silly wabbit." Bill opened his eyes to find a boy standing next to his bed. "I know you, little man."

"Hey, Santa Bunny."

"You got your hair back, José. You look so healthy."

"You don't."

"I know. But I've been worse. I wish I could get up out of this bed."

"I know. That's why I'm here."

"What do you mean?"

"You remember that night you and Pat gave me the signed Steve Young poster, and my necklace."

"Oh, I do remember that. Where are those things now?"

"With Mamá and Papá who live with Aunt Maria."

"Good for them." Bill smiled.

"Anyway, do you remember the last Christmas in the Payson hospital, when I wanted to give you and Squeaky a Christmas present? You told me to find something that didn't cost money?"

"That's right. You wanted to make us happy, even though you were so very sick from your chemo.

"After you and Squeaky left my hospital room, I asked Jesus to let me do something special for you, you know, as a present."

"Oh?"

"Can I give you my present now?"

"Sure. But are those tears, I see? Are you sad, José?"

"No, happy." José took Bill's hand, and pulled him up to the sitting position in the bed. He then pulled the ragged tan blanket off and flung it onto the floor. Doc's legs slid around to the side of the bed. "Let's go, Doc. I'm supposed to deliver you to somebody very special." José pulled him to his feet. *Clump!* The bucket fell to the floor. Bill and José both looked down into it.

"Squeaky clean, huh, Doc?"

"Yeah." Bill mused at the symbolism of that phrase—squeaky clean. He knelt in front of José. Thank you, José. You freed me from my suffering in that bed."

"Doc," José smiled. "Don't you get it?"

"Get what?"

"All those medical things, all those gifts, all your love to me and my family, you freed me from so much suffering, too. When Jesus told me about how you were going to get real sick, I asked to help him make you better."

"What did he say to that?"

"He told me I could help, and I could bring you back to the person you love the most." José squeezed Doc around the neck.

A beam of light surged in from above. At first they shielded their eyes, but it grew softer as it grew brighter. Bill looked back to see the bucket and hospital bed disappear. In an instant, all his suffering disappeared as though a thousand shackles had been unloosed from his body. Peace, relief, and joy filled his soul.

They reached the end of the tunnel. José walked Bill through a beautiful meadow of flowers and tall grasses, up a small hill, and across a narrow path.

"Bill!" Pat reached out with both hands.

"Pat? Pat, it is you." Bill's heart swelled. José walked up and placed Bill's hands into Pat's. They looked into each others eyes, then embraced each other. "I can't tell you in words how much I love you, Pat."

"I love you, too, Bill."

"Now, Squeaky and Santa Bunny can be together forever." José hugged their legs.

"Thank you, José." Pat caressed his hair. "You brought my best friend home to me."

"Merry Christmas, Squeaky and Santa Bunny." José looked up to them, eyes gleaming. "I want to tell you how much you mean to me. After my last chemo in the Payson hospital, I thought I might not live through the night." José took their hands. "Then you danced into my room with those gifts. It gave me hope. Hey, after I met Steve Young, I lived for two more years. Then I shared my hope with other children in the cancer center. The one's who were meant to live on are still alive because of it."

"José, that is so precious." Pat knelt down.

"Yes, we're so glad you told us." Bill knelt, too.

"Muchas gracias, Santa and Squeaky." José hugged their necks, then walked away.

"De nada," they replied.

"Hey, José, will we see you again?" Bill asked.

"I think so. I help the children in the cancer center, kinda like Pat helped you, but I'll be around."

"Te amo mucho, amigo." Bill and Pat waved.

"Te amo, Squeaky and Doc. I mean Santa Bunny." José disappeared down the path.

They stood hand in hand. Bill looked into Pat's eyes. Tears streamed down her cheeks. "Are those angel tears I see?"

Pat wiped them with her hand. "José was right, you know. We'll be together forever now."

"I'm so glad, too. Being alone, without you and my family, was like hell to me."

"How do you feel now, Sweetheart?"

"So full of joy, I can hardly contain it."

"Oh, Bill, you'll have to get used to that. It feels like this all the time up here." Pat leaned into his chest. Bill lifted her, twirling her in a complete circle.

"Bill, we're not alone."

"No?"

"No, I brought some people you haven't seen for a while." Pat turned Bill around into the embrace of his father, his mother, his mother and father-in law, José's grandparents, and many other family and friends who were there to greet him. The reunion added immeasurable joy to his already overflowing heart.

Eventually, Pat and Bill walked alone in a beautiful garden. All the fruit trees blossomed. All of their favorite flowers bloomed by the thousands—the orchids, roses, lilacs, snapdragons, tulips, honeysuckles, and more.

"Pat?"

"Yes."

"This is such a peaceful place.

"It really is. I love it here."

"I'm trying to sort some things out."

"Can I help?"

"My body laid in a hospital bed for years, but at the end there, I went all over Payson with you. How is that possible?"

"In the last few moments of life, the line between being in and out of the body almost completely disappears."

"Oh."

"Do you have another question?"

"Well, yes. You looked so young when you came to my hospital room. You look young now."

"So do you. You look the same as you did the day I met you."

"I know. How is that? I mean, how can we look this young, yet we died so very old?"

"I had the same question when I first arrived here. As I understand it, who we really are is not just about being alive in a mortal body. We are eternally young. It's just our mortal bodies that age."

"That makes sense." Bill looked down at his feet.

"Something else on your mind?"

"May I ask a difficult question?" Bill hesitated but really needed an answer.

"Certainly."

"When you left us, it was sudden."

"Yes, it was."

"Well, why couldn't I go suddenly, too?" Bill fixed his eyes on Pat's.

"Some questions don't have easy answers." Pat stood and looked away.

"Don't you want to tell me?"

"I do. I guess I'm concerned about how you might take it."

"Sit next to me, here, Pat."

She sat back down.

"Please tell me what in the world was I supposed to get out of that terrible suffering in the darkness?"

"It wasn't what you got out of it."

"No?"

"No. It was what Jacob got out of it."

"I don't understand."

"You see, after I left, Jacob desperately needed you. He needed his dad."

"But I wasn't really there for him. In fact, I hurt them a great deal during my sickness."

"Even so, you being hurtful, sick, and bothersome meant that you were still around. To Jacob a sick dad was better than no dad at all."

"So I suffered for Jacob's sake?"

"That's right. You suffered so that Jacob could get used to us being gone. It's the only way it would have worked for him."

"Oh." Bill rubbed his chin.

"Had we both gone suddenly, Jacob could not have healed as he just did. Your lingering opened the door for his grief to come out. It was the only way for us to move on and for Jacob to let us go."

"I see," Bill whispered.

"Are you all right?" Pat took his hand.

"I am." Bill stood. "I would never had chosen to suffer in the darkness for my own sake. But I'd do it again for Jacob's sake. I'd do anything for him."

"I know you would." Pat looked into his eyes, smiling.

"What?"

"I like talking to you, here, in such a lovely place."

"Me, too."

"Any more questions?"

"Well, I have wondered about Elizabeth. How are she and her husband?"

"They live in Vancouver, with their triplet girls."

"Triplets?"

"Yes, and they are all doing fine. I stop by to make sure of it from time to time."

"Triplets," Bill mused aloud. Pat put her arm around his waist. He put his on her shoulder. They walked together down the path.

"Hey, look over there, it's Nadia." Pat pointed down the pathway at the garden's edge.

"Nadia." Bill reached out to shake her hand as she approached. "Thank you for all you did for me."

"My pleasure."

"What's that in your hands?"

"Well, Bill, I have a letter for the two of you." Nadia handed the scroll to Bill.

"Letter? From whom?" Bill asked as he slid the ribbon off the scroll and opened it.

"From, Raphael," Nadia smiled, placing her arms behind her back.

"Raphael? Who's Raphael?" Bill looked to Pat for an answer.

"He's the chief guardian angel, the one who assigned me and Nadia to help you. Go on, read it, Bill," Pat urged.

"It says . . ."

Pat and Bill Wilson,
You both are officially called to serve together as guardian angels
to the Jacob, Nancy, and Shelly Wilson Family. You shall report
immediately to the Christmas cabin at Payson lakes
for the duration of their Christmas vacation.
Special note: Shelly and Jacob will be sledding and
you will be needed more than once to keep them safe.

"How did Shelly say it? Wahoo! We get to work together, Bill!" Pat cheered.

"Thank the Lord." Bill kissed her cheek.

"Hey wait, there's more," said Nadia.

"There is?" Pat looked over Bill's shoulder.

"It says . . ."

You are both also officially called to be a team of community therapists
to serve with Nadia in the Richards Family recovery.
Report to my station with Nadia after the Wilsons return to Payson.
Raphael

"The Richards family?" Bill handed the scroll to Pat.

"You know, the young man with brain damage from the motorcycle accident. His room sat next to the Christmas tree down the hall from yours," Nadia explained. "That's right. He really got hurt, didn't he?"

"His entire family is hurt, not just because of his accident."

"How can we help?"

"Yes, how?" Pat handed the scroll back to Nadia.

"I'll fill in the details later. You two better get down to the cabin."

"Thanks, Nadia." Pat took Bill's hand and snapped her fingers. They instantly arrived in the kitchen.

"Hey, can you teach me how to do that?"

"Later." She pointed to Jacob, who just handed the note to Nancy.

"How sweet." Nancy whispered. "And you know, I think Pat did come last night. It felt as though she were right here with us. But how did she help Bill?" Nancy reread the note.

"I can't say, but I'll tell you one thing, I felt much closer to my dad in the hospital yesterday. It was like, somehow, in spite of Alzheimer's and all the other problems, he heard me. He really knew my pain and helped me get through it."

Ring, ring. Their old black circular dial phone pierced the calm. Jacob reached over to answer it.

"Hello, yes, this is Bill Wilson's son. Yes, I am Jacob Wilson." Jacob paused and took Nancy's hand. "He did? Peacefully, a few minutes ago?" Nancy placed her arms gently around Jacob's waist. "Yes, thank you for calling the mortuary. So there's nothing more we need to do there today? Thank you. Goodbye." Jacob dropped his head to his chest as he placed the old headset back onto its mount.

"I am so very sorry, Jacob."

"No, no, Nancy. Don't feel sorry." Jacob turned to face her. "I don't. I just feel joy that Dad is free from that horrible disease." I'm not crying tears of sadness. I'm full of joy that I spent the time yesterday, making my peace with him. Jacob put his arm around her shoulders.

"Bill," Pat whispered. Bill didn't hear. He felt caught up in Jacob's reaction. He now sensed Jacob would start living his life as a husband and daddy again. "Bill, let's go chat with Shelly." Pat snapped her fingers and they stood upstairs next to Shelly's bed. They had a short conversation with her, then Pat snapped again. They stood behind the couch.

"Hee, hee. Yes, I did." Jacob and Nancy looked up to the ceiling as Shelly giggled.

"Shelly loves to talk to her Jim and Chrissy doll. Do you hear her carrying on up there?" Nancy and Jacob turned off the stove and walked into the living room to the couch.

"She has such a bright imagination, doesn't she?"

"She does."

"Nancy, these last few years have been hard on you. Instead of turning to you and facing my challenges with you, I shut you and Shelly out and made things even harder. I hope you can forgive me?" Jacob's sorrowful eyes revealed his feelings.

"I already have forgiven you."

"Thank you, friend."

"He's going to be fine, Pat." Bill whispered.

"Thanks a great deal to you."

"I'm his dad. It's what dads do . . . kinda."

"You know," Nancy said, "isn't this what Christmas is about—forgiving the bad things and working harder for the good things."

"Yeah."

"Jacob, this has been our best Christmas ever!"

"Yeah."

"Hee, hee, hee. Yes, and Grandmom left us all these wonderful presents," Shelly reported. They all looked up at the ceiling. Pat gave Bill a squeeze. He raised his eyebrows.

"She takes after you, Jacob." Nancy chided.

"Somehow, she takes after her grandmom more," he replied as Nancy rested her head on his shoulder.

"Yes, you should have seen it here last night." Shelly continued. "There was food and presents, and oh, yes, Grandmom came. He was? Granddad was here, too?"

Nancy and Jacob jumped to their feet, their mouths wide opened.

"Please don't go so soon." Shelly begged. "Yes, I have it right here. I'll remember. Okay. Goodbye." Shelly's little feet pitter-patted across the wooden floor to the top of the stairs. They watched her as she descended.

"Good morning, Mommy." Shelley skipped across the living room to the table and climbed up to her place. "Good morning, Daddy. Are we sledding today?" Jacob and Nancy walked over to join her.

"Good morning, Shelly and yes, we are," he replied.

"Where are your Chrissy and Jim dolls? Weren't you just talking to them upstairs?" Nancy pointed up.

"Yes, but they had to go. I won't be talking to them much. They have some other things to do together."

"Oh, thank goodness." Nancy smiled in relief.

"Yes, thank goodness." Jacob sighed.

"This is my new friend. We just had a great chat up stairs. He had to go, too, but he'll be back." Shelly took the baby Jesus figurine from her apron pocket and placed it on the table. Jacob's mouth fell wide open again. Nancy's eyes grew larger. "Can we have special syrup this morning?"